The Testimony of Sal Madge

John Little

© 2020 John Little

All rights reserved

No part of this publication may be reproduced, stored in a retrieval system, stored in a database and/or published in any form or by any means, electronic, mechanical, photocopying, recording or otherwise, without the prior written permission of the publisher.

ISBN 9781677185115

To the memory of my mother
Who was Muriel Gordon
A Whitehaven lass

Glossary

Thou: (you) pronounced thoo. Long or short depending on context
Thee: (your) really thy, pronounced thi
Stife: smoke
Louping: jumping
Yan: one
Marra: mate
Wuk: work
Bait: lunch/food (bite)
Nivver: never
Alloo: allow
Ga: go
Hest: hast (have to)
Nut; not
Hed: had
Laal: little/small
Radge: crazy person, maniac
Agyan: again
Sin: seen
Ah've: I've
Frae: from
Biddy: louse
Gimmer: older female sheep
Thissen: yourself
What fettle? how are you?
Asser Marra? how are you mate?
Yat: gate
Vanya: very near
Scop a feuw styans: throw a few stones
Maff: hermaphrodite
Yat; Gate or door

Preface

Memory is a curious thing in that what one generation thinks memorable turns into something that is tenuous and hard to get a grip on. In particular, there are names attached to people in history that conjure up images of what they did, but which turn out to be myth or mere fabrication. Tales of Robin Hood or William Wallace spring to mind. My hometown, Whitehaven, has such a figure in the personage of Sal Madge who was a woman living in the nineteenth century. She dressed in manly fashion above the waist, wore a skirt and did not pretend to be a man; yet lived her life with what many these days would call 'masculine privilege.' In the context of her times, she did things that only men were supposed to do; she stayed single, drank pints, chewed tobacco, smoked a pipe and could hold her own in fighting or wrestling against male opponents. Her life, in folk memory, has turned her into a sort of celebrity in that most people living in the area know her name and are familiar with the facts set out above.

The surprising thing about her is that, although she lived only a century or so ago, there is very little known of her, most of it dating from the eulogies and obituaries written about her after she had gone. The internet yields not a lot and much of it is the same matter, recycled. Not surprisingly, she remains the subject of much speculation; some folk think she was a man, but since her details are available from her birth in the Penrith workhouse right through the censuses that took place all her life, this idea does not hold water. Sarah Madgin was a woman, not a 'molly' (a male transvestite) and that fact was attested in court by one of Whitehaven's leading solicitors.

I have also seen speculation that she was a 'maff' (hermaphrodite) or a lesbian. It may well be that she was; if so, then it was quite an achievement for her to gain such respect and fame as she did in her community. For a working class woman who liked women to prosper in a male dominated society would have been extraordinarily difficult. The Whitehaven she lived in was not an open and liberal sort of place; to some extent it was tribal. The Orange and Green tribes were particularly strong, yet Sal Madge lived among Protestants and Catholics who held strong religious beliefs, and she swam among them like a fish in water, apparently with universal respect. No priest or pastor thundered against her for unnatural behaviour or bad example: quite to the contrary for she was held in great esteem, even being on joking terms with the Yellow Earl.

To be clear, there is not one shred of evidence extant about her sexuality; not one tittle, as a certain solicitor would have said. This being so, I have not made her into something she may not have been, but placed what I have found into the narrative. You must make up your own mind, but I have treated her as I would think of an asexual person, in that I surmise that she was not interested in the whole business. Considering the life of the average working class woman at that time I find this very understandable.

Many of the core events I have placed into this novel are real. Some are made up and it may be hard to discern which are fiction and which are fact. Surprising though it may be, the incident described in chapter one is quite true, though I have of course embellished it. Others are not real, though within the limits of plausibility are based on what I have read. Sal Madge did not hesitate to enforce her will by use of her strength; that is true enough, so forgive me if I show her doing just that.

However, there is one thing I have discovered and I think I know why Sal Madge is famous. Without giving anything away, there are very few men, or women who are brave enough to do what Sal Madge did, in real life, at the Connelly house in Rosemary Lane in 1887. The sheer raw courage to pull off something like that is astonishing; I am not sure that I would have done it, or most of the people reading this now. If it had not been for two drunks muddying the waters, I am quite certain that she and her marra, John Kennedy, would have been given some kind of award for bravery. I have no idea what motive Parker and Walker had for what they did, but the sequence leading to Carlisle gaol was real enough. I do know who Whitehaven believed though, because it was not their names that went down in folk memory with such esteem and their coffins were not followed to the cemetery by thousands.

I can find no newspaper references to Sal Madge before 1887 and I am content with the thought that the events outlined in this book are the main reason for her local fame. Her actions in Rosemary Lane raised her from being a local 'character' into something rather more special which commanded great honour in the town. The respect and kudos that must have come her way after she risked her life as she did, must have been tremendous; a real life working class heroine.

The process of researching was also rewarding in that I was able to discover more about another local hero, not so well known; Mr Edward Atter, solicitor at law, whose services kept many people who could not afford legal help out of prison. I have no doubt that Whitehaven's history holds many other interesting characters, but this man was someone who worked for the good of the community and a lot of Whitehaven families owe recognition to his memory too.

It has been my aim to try to place Sal Madge into the Whitehaven of her day and to do it with as much respect as I can. I have not made her into something she was not, and have tried to keep to what I know she was. My prime objective is to enable my readers to stand in the shoes of people long dead and see their world as they saw it. That is how I judge my own success or failure.

Dialect is always a vexed question in dealing with books set in particular regions. Sal Madge and her friends would all have spoken with distinct west Cumberland and Whitehaven accents. There are subtle variations throughout the region. The sing-song cadence of West Cumbrian speech is quite musical, and with its flattened vowels and upturned pitch at the end of sentences is not possible to duplicate in writing. I must ask pardon for inconsistencies in speech but have borne in mind that my book may be read outside West Cumbria and any more attempts at dialect than I have included, may not be understood by many people. 'Thou' as spoken in my family was always 'thoo' but cut slightly short. 'Thee' was 'thi'. I have chosen not to attempt full dialect but to sprinkle a few words in here and there. My intention was to make clear that my characters did not speak with standard BBC English; if it does not ring true then I can only ask that you suspend your disbelief and hear it in your mind as it should be.

I wish to thank my wife, Ruth, and David Banks of Beechville, Nova Scotia, for their painstaking proof reading work. My local beta readers were Laura Palmer, Betty Telford, Hazel Block, Alan Irwin at the Beacon museum and Chris Shackley and I owe them thanks, particularly for their points on local dialect and geography. Beta readers for a wider audience were Irene Martin in Fife and Eunice Small in Kent, Claire Ball in Bristol and Kate Roxburgh in London. Thanks must also go to Kerry McLaughlin at the Beacon for her assistance. The photograph on the front cover is document reference (PH/704) and is used by permission of Robert Baxter, Senior Archivist at the Cumbria Archive and local studies centre in Whitehaven where it may be found. Mr Baxter also acted as a beta reader. I am also grateful to RS Parker of Whitehaven for information about Edward Atter and allowing me to see his face. Other people who helped were Tony Calvin, Peter Franklin, Geoff Everitt, Joe Ritson, Alan Cleaver, Michael Todd and Helen Rogan. I am thankful for the use of a wide range of source books including Daniel Hay's excellent *Whitehaven; an illustrated history,* Michael and Sylvia Moon's *Bygone Whitehaven* series. Colin McCourt's *Newhouses revisited* was very useful as were several of Alan Routledge's works. Without the British Newspaper Archives I would never have been able to find out what it was that brought Sal Madge into a courtroom in 1887 and how the formidable Mr Atter used his legal skills with such crushing effect. Any readers wishing to follow up the newspaper source material will find that the inquest and the trial were covered very well in *The Cumberland Pacquet* and *The Whitehaven News,* as well as receiving syndicated mentions in newspapers across the United Kingdom.

Finally, I hope you enjoy reading the book as much as I did writing it. Just remember; it is not a history book. It is a novel based on truth and real people. Thus, there is much of fiction and speculation about it, but if it enables you to know Sal Madge, Edward Atter, and the Whitehaven of their day better, then I can only be glad.

John Little, January 2020

Chapter 1

A Strong Minded Woman

The wind hustled its way across the south harbour, cold, peppery with sleet and insistently cutting. Those who had to be abroad about their business in this darkening evening of early February 1887 shivered, and made their way home thinking of their dinners. Around the periphery of the harbour the force of the breeze was broken by the warehouses, taverns, bawdy houses and offices fronting the quay, and it filtered into the older parts of the town through ancient cobbled alleys and dishevelled houses, replete with the dirt of ages and the debris of the working day. Small flakes of snow danced their way into the dim yellow light of the oil lamp part way up Bardywell Lane and settled to melt their existence into the black slime in the central gutter. The lane headed uphill towards the crowded rookeries of Mount Pleasant and the High Road, but up along the slope, just before it became very steep, was a low dirty looking public house called the Manx Arms.

Through the flaking door set into a row of down at heel three storey terraced houses was a single room bar, and a visitor on entering would see a rough counter of planks over barrels behind which were a few kegs of beer, for this was an ale house on the edge of one of the poorest parts of town. There was nothing fancy to drink here. In a corner of the room two labourers were drinking pints of dark beer; They were obviously from the pottery at the Ginns, as their clay-slip stained clothes proclaimed, and had not been home to change before calling in for a few drinks. A woman bar-keeper was polishing some glasses with a rag, and in the other corner, near a small coal fire sat what appeared to be an ordinary working man in a flat cap puffing contentedly on a short clay pipe, also drinking strong ale. On the table was a deck of cards and it was plain that this individual was waiting for some companions to arrive and play a few hands of Loo or Whist. The face of this personage was nut brown as of someone who spent a lot of time out of doors, none too clean, and seamed with the wrinkles of hard work, smoking and drinking. It could not be called a handsome face, and indeed there were many who thought it downright ugly; not a few feared it, and with good reason. The hair of this customer was cut short at the back, but not too short, longer at the sides and the dark brown eyes were those of an old soul, full of the acquired wisdom of 56 years; the gaze was frank and direct. It was a hard face and not one for tomfoolery. A dirty kerchief round the neck, and a closely buttoned woollen jacket with a waistcoat completed the view that could be seen above the table. Human beings all have a smell, and even more so in this part of town where work was dirty and hard; this particular person smelled very strongly of horse with undertones of old sweat and tobacco. Only if the eye looked downwards would an observer have cause to change their mind, for instead of the expected scuffed and dirty trousers of the ordinary working man and a pair of stout clogs, there was a skirt. It was not just any skirt either for it was thick, stiff with dirt, innumerable stains of indeterminate origin and as stout as armour. The card player waiting for her friends was a woman. At her feet sat a small red-brown mongrel with floppy ears and soulful eyes called Flirt who was her constant companion.

The warm fug of the bar-room was abruptly disturbed by the door being shoved open and four men entered, loud, evidently already with a few drinks under their belts. Each wore a thick dark pea-jacket crusted with old salt-stains, woollen caps and the one among them who appeared to be their leader sported a very old cheese-cutter cap that had seen better days. From the look of them they were sailors just in from one of the dozens of sailing ships in the harbour. Colliers from Whitehaven sailed all round the coast, over to Belfast and to places much further afield, carrying some of the best coal in the world. Tramp cargo ships from all round Europe called in here too. Their crews had a reputation for being tough. Disreputable and living life to the full when they got their pay and came ashore, this group had evidently just been paid and they were on a 'randy', determined to get as drunk as possible as quickly as they could.

'Ay-up, pints of your best Missus and don't take your time about it.'

'Coming right up,' said the barwoman and began to pour the first pint from a barrel. One of the other men spied out the best table near the fire, already occupied by the singular looking woman and gave out a drunken and disbelieving guffaw. The barwoman looked up sharply, 'You've not been here before have you?'

'No Missus,' said the leader. 'We got blown in here heading for Belfast.'

'Well,' said the barwoman in a whisper, 'you'd better tell your friends not to mess with that one. That's Sal Madge.'

'What one?' The leader looked round to see the woman sitting at the table by the fire. She was not looking aside or trying not to be seen, but her eyes were on him, calm, puffing at her pipe and apparently wholly unperturbed. Instantly, she became the funniest thing that he had ever seen and he began to laugh, as did his other companions.

'Hahaha! Oh dear my poor sides; I've not seen the likes of you before! What do you think lads, is it some sort of monkey?'

'Is that a dog or a bitch?' shouted another one derisively, pointing at the terrier.

'Oh bloody hellfire,' said the barwoman setting down the glass she was holding, and she disappeared out of the back door, bolting it from the other side as she left. At the same time, the two men who had been quietly drinking gulped the rest of their beer down and went out the front door in haste.

'Is it a man or a woman?' asked one of the drunks, very loudly.

'I don't know mate. The barmaid said it was Sal Madge so I'm guessing it's a woman.'

'What are you, man or woman?'

'Ugly bugger, whatever he or she is.'

'Look at the face on that!'

'That's a woman? I'm asking you, would you ever?'

'Not even with a paper bag over its head!'

'Haha, yes you would. You'd have owt in a skirt.'

'Not that I wouldn't. It stinks an' all.'

All of this time the woman at the table had not altered her stance, merely looking at the men barracking her with a glittering reptilian eye, but now she reached a decision and got up.

'Aye aye; she's going lads.'

'Well we'll have the best table then.'

'I think we should find out if it's a man or a woman.'

'Leaving are you, darling? Sure you won't stop and have a drink?'

By this time the woman had reached the door and stopped. The man who wanted to find out what sex she was before she left was walking towards her, his arm stretched out to grab her shoulder, but stopped when she reached out and pulled the bolt so that no one could get into the room. The face of the man who had intended to touch her now changed dramatically, from mockery to uncertainty. This did not last long as she strolled calmly over to him and brought her knee hard up into his groin. As he screamed with the pain of it and doubled over she grabbed his head as it came down and rammed it hard onto a table. He went out like a light.

'Balls,' said Sal Madge. 'They're your weak point, every one of you. Now who's next?'

'I ain't taking that from no woman,' said one of the men and grabbed a bottle from the bar as he headed towards her. His advance was met with a sideswipe from a chair that sent him sprawling. Then she turned towards the other two advancing at her, one of whom became occupied in other matters as Flirt sprang up and fixed his teeth in the man's buttocks. He yelled in pain as Sal's hard fist took his companion full on the nose, crunching it flat; all Hell broke loose as she reached down and grabbed between his legs. She had a crushing grip like a vice and he screamed in pure agony as she lifted him up by his crotch.

The barwoman, who was quite a heavy lady, had in the meantime, run at a waddling pace and was sweating profusely and gasping by the time she reached the harbour. There she saw dimly along the quay to where the pier known as the Lime Tongue jutted out towards the sea, there was a tall figure in a distinctive peaked cap strolling along the edge. As she paused to collect her breath a dirty black locomotive came down the harbour railway from William Pit to the north, pulling a line of coal wagons towards the staithes down on the West Strand. With the noise of the puffing and the clank of the wagons there was no chance that she could be heard, and the train now intervened between her and the policeman she sought. As the last wagon passed a cloud of smoke obscured her view, but as it cleared the figure of PC Beattie became visible and the barwoman's relief was palpable.

'Help! Mr Beattie. Help!'

Thomas Beattie had been enjoying a quiet evening thus far; it was early yet, and it was a Monday. Some of the locals spent much of their time drunk, but there had been no trouble. However, like all of Whitehaven's policemen he was used to having to react very quickly. He recognised the barwoman straight away as someone he had regular dealings with, or rather whose troublesome customers he had dealt with.

'What's up Mrs Simon; what's fashing thou?'

'It's Sal Madge Mr Beattie. There's four sailors in the bar asking if she's a man or a woman.'

'Bloody Hell!' exclaimed the policeman. 'She'll murder them! Not local lads then?'

'No Mr Beattie; strangers.'

'Dead and buried strangers if I don't get up there,' replied the policeman and set off at a brisk trot, drawing his truncheon as he ran. As he entered Bardywell Lane he heard shouting and screaming with shrieks of anguish and the crash of breaking furniture, but the voices were male; one of them was crying, 'Help murder!' Reaching the door of the Manx Arms, surmounted by a large sign with the three armoured and spurred legs emblem of the Isle of Man, he hammered on the door. Someone on the inside seemed to be trying to claw the door open to escape.

'Open up Sal. It's PC Beattie.'

There was one final despairing wail from inside the pub and a crash then all was silent. Beattie wasted no more time, but put his shoulder to the door. He was a big man; the door was old, as was the bolt, so it flew open on the third try. Sal Madge was sitting quietly back at her table; her pipe had gone out so she was chewing a quid of tobacco. As Beattie came in she spat expertly into a spittoon by the bar. Three men lay unconscious in various parts of the room and the fourth one was just coming to, moaning slightly. Apart from Sal's all the other tables were over-turned. Two chairs were lying wrecked in splinters on the floor. As the barwoman came in and looked at the mess Sal nodded at a purse lying on the bar and said,

'I'm sorry about the mess Mrs Simon, but them chaps has just been paid. They started it so I reckon they can pay for it.'

'I think you'd better stay here Sal while I sort this out.'

'I'm not going anywhere Thomas. I came in here for a quiet drink and a game of cards and that's what I'm here to do.'

For the next few minutes the barwoman and PC Beattie were engaged in reviving the unconscious sailors. Sal lit her pipe again and gazed at the scene with an almost benevolent expression on her face. Eventually all the casualties had come round; none of them needed attention at the infirmary and apart from cuts, bruises and aches in their nether regions they would recover.

'I want her arrested,' said the ringleader of the sailors.

'On what grounds do I arrest her?' replied Beattie.

'She assaulted us. She did us grievous bodily harm.'

Beattie looked at him quizzically, 'Did she now?'

'Aye she bloody did; just look at us.'

The policeman looked at him deliberately and then at his companions.

'Yes, you do seem to have suffered grievous bodily harm; contusions, wounds, blood. Yes, definitely fits the description of grievous bodily harm under the act of 1861; whoever did this should be arrested, put on trial and undoubtedly would be sentenced to a period of penal servitude.'

The sailor looked puzzled.

'It means prison with hard labour.'

'Ah; well I want her arrested for grievous bodily harm.'

Beattie's face assumed a wooden expression. Yes sir, I shall arrest her and take her to the police station where she will be charged and will appear at the police court tomorrow. The seriousness of the offence being such as it is, I imagine she will have to go for trial at the assizes in Carlisle. Open and shut case.'

Sal Madge's face held no expression.

The sailor was jubilant, 'Arrest her then!'

'I will sir. You'll have to give evidence of course. You and your friends.'

'But you know what happened here.'

'No, I don't, sir. I know what appears to have happened, but I was not in the room. The weight placed on my evidence would be very light. I have no doubt that the local solicitor, Mr Edward Atter, will appear for the defence and he is very hot on evidence is Mr Atter. You will have to appear in front of him: and at the assizes.'

'But our ship will have sailed by the end of the week.'

'No matter sir, I imagine the court will issue a *subpoena*.'

'What's that?'

'Well it's a notice to you, sir, from the court. You would have to attend on penalty of arrest.'

'I'm not sure I like that Bill,' interrupted one of the other men.

'Then of course there's the events of this evening as they appear in court.'

'The events?'

'Oh yes, sir. They come out quite detailed in court. Four strapping rough men, one woman of no great size. She locks the door and beats the four of them unconscious. Shouldn't be surprised if it makes the national newspapers.'

'Here you can't do that; we'd be a laughing stock.'

Constable Beattie had his notebook out by now and looked down his nose at the speaker.

'Can't be helped. You'll be famous on every ship that sails the seven seas. The lads who had their blocks knocked off by an old lass. Well that's lady justice for you and she must be served.'

The sailors by now were looking thoroughly alarmed. One of them shouted at the ringleader, 'I don't want anything to do with this Bill. You leave me out of this; I'm off.'

The other two looked at each other askance and turned to go, 'You're on your own Bill. Best leave this one alone.'

Bill looked at PC Beattie and licked his lips, and his eyes could not meet those of the officer.

'Look, can't we just forget about this? I mean life wouldn't be worth living. You know that.'

'Oh I know that sir, but justice is blind to such things. No, if charges are pressed then it will all have to come out.'

'Do charges have to be pressed?'

'Why no sir; not in this case. If the offended party does not press charges then there is nothing I can do. The matter would have to drop.'

'Then I don't want to press charges.'

'Ah, very well sir. There is, of course, the question of the damage done here; the smashed chairs.'

'I didn't smash them. She did.'

Beattie looked at the barwoman, 'Civil case I fear, Mrs Simon. You must go to court to recover the money.'

'Alright. Alright,' shouted the exasperated sailor, 'How much?'

'Five bob should cover it,' replied the barwoman.

'Daylight bloody robbery!' said the sailor, but nonetheless he took the purse which was his own off the bar and paid the money with a bad grace.

'No need to swear so,' said the policeman, 'Ladies present.'

The sailor muttered something very nasty under his breath and left.

Beattie looked at Sal Madge.

'They asked for it.'

'They did; and they got it.'

'You should watch it, Sal. You've been lucky. If he'd wanted to press charges I would have had to arrest you and all that I said would have happened.'

'Aye, I know. But it didn't did it?'

'No, but you've a good name in town; try and keep it that way.'

'I've only ever thumped people who needed thumping.'

'I'll allow that is true, but keep your nose clean.'

Sal Madge laughed, 'That's a difficult thing to ask in my case.' She shook with laughter at what was evidently a huge joke. Beattie turned to the barwoman and nodded, heading for the door.

'Thomas.'

'It's PC Beattie Sal. I'm on duty.'

'Don't be daft. I've known thee all the days of thy life and thy mam and dad before. I won't forget this. I owe thee.'

Beattie gave a wry smile, then he went out of the door to resume his beat down by the cold docks. On his way he touched his cap to a tall figure in a top hat picking his way over the lines and heading towards the steps leading up to Mount Pleasant. Any other man he would have advised to turn back for the Mount was unsafe during the day, let alone at night; unlit and full of bad characters to whom assault and robbery were second nature. This man, however, was as safe as he would be sitting at his own dining table; Mr Edward Atter, solicitor at law, passed safely on his way and went wherever he liked with the assurance of a man guarded by a squad of infantry.

Sal Madge refilled her pipe again as the barwoman called her husband who had just come in to set about repairing the bolt and sat waiting for her usual companions. They were not long in coming; soon John Connelly, blacksmith, John Kennedy, coalminer, and various members of the Madge clan who lived in the same row of houses as Sal up at Windmill on the High Road in Kells were gathered round the table. Shortly afterwards they were joined by Isaac Tyson, a colliery under-manager at Wellington Pit, who had known Sal since childhood, more of whom, later. They listened to the tale of what had happened, but fighting and drunks were common currency in this area and they themselves often numbered among the offenders so the cards and beer were of more interest to them than Sal flooring some sailors. It had happened before, and probably would again.

'The fact is Sal,' said Isaac, who knew her better than most,

'Them fellas was lucky. You let 'em off light.'

'Aye well, I'm in a good mood today.'

It was true; the sailors had no major broken bones, nor smashed skulls; not even dislocated jaws though one of them would have to have his nose pulled back into place; they had been a minor diversion, now best forgotten in favour of better things. In here it was warm, convivial, nicely smelly and friendly; far better than being at home for most of them; therefore, enjoy the night.

Chapter 2

Sal Madge

In Sal's life Isaac Tyson was a name to conjure with, because she had known him ever since she had moved to Whitehaven from Penrith at the age of five. She and Isaac had both been living in the Mount Pleasant area at that time, though nowadays he had bettered himself and was living in a house in Chapel Street with his wife Elizabeth and four children. It was quite a change from their old haunts. Mount Pleasant had originally been a well-designed set of workers' houses for its day, but now they were half a century old and had not been the subject of any maintenance since the day the builders moved out. They had no privies, though a few of them did have an ash pit in the tiny yard that separated their back wall from the hillside they were cut into. Most had nothing since the back wall of the long terrace was built into the hill and damp seeped through it into the houses. In theory any ash or human waste was deposited in dunghills at the end of each terrace, which would be taken away each week by scavenger carts in the employ of Lord Lonsdale who owned most of the town, but these were long terraces and many occupants could not be bothered to go the distance, especially in bad weather. In addition there were only four scavengers employed to cover the whole of the town and two carts; they could not be everywhere so concentrated on the centre of town. The narrow lanes between the terraces which rose steeply up the hill were thus deep in human waste, ash and all sorts of debris that had to be threaded through in order to stay reasonably clean underfoot. Occasionally the scavengers would come in and scrape the streets, a process done only when it was worthwhile doing; the dirt, being rich in manure and rotting stuff, was taken away to fertilise the fields of his lordship's farms and grow good wheat and potatoes. The area stank of rotting vegetable material, human excreta and animal waste of several kinds. Quite a few people kept a pig and their styes added to the general odour. In the winter the liquid part of the waste soaked through walls into peoples' houses and made yellow crystals, mould and green slime on the inside walls. In the summer, dry waste would blow about in the wind. Not surprisingly fevers of all kinds flourished, and outbreaks of cholera and typhus were not rare. Amongst this dirt five year old Sarah Madgin had played with four year old Isaac Tyson from a few doors down and it was he who could not be bothered to call her by her full name. 'Sal Madge' was what he called her and it stuck and became what everyone called her. Indeed it was so such a useful shortening of the name that the whole family took to using it as their actual name.

The young Sal did not live in a house. The old nail maker's workshop the family inhabited was a cavern hewn out of the hillside, lined with cut stone and divided into two chambers, one of which was occupied by grandfather and the other by Mary Madgin, her new husband John Steel and his new family; Sal and her brother Thomas. It was this stark fact which was to shape Sal's existence and her outlook on life. Their home was entered through a door that opened onto the lane and once inside a visitor would step onto a dirt floor made of earth rammed hard and kept as clean as possible by Sal's mother, who swept it constantly. Though the walls let damp through, the inside was dry for most of the time as the nail makers had driven a chimney shaft down through the slope above; coal was plentiful in Whitehaven and did not need to be bought if you knew where to go. In some places it could be dug out of the earth, though for many families it was easier to set the children to hunting for coal on the slag heaps, the mine spoil heaps, or on the sea shore to find sea coal or 'smush' which was washed up from coal deposits offshore. Inside was dark, rather smelly, but warm. The family could not afford candles, but occasionally used rush-lights and assiduously saved the fat from any meat they had specifically for this purpose.

Like all residents of the Mount Pleasant area, Sal's family fought a never-ending battle against fleas, nits and lice. They were so much part of life that they did not find these vermin at all unusual, but Sarah found them irritating. As soon as she was able to do it for herself, and to her mother's distress, she had taken a pair of scissors and cut her blonde hair short and parted it down one side in imitation of the boys she knew in the street. Finding it easier to comb her head that way, and also that it fitted with her nature, she insisted on keeping it like that. In her this did not look strange because in character, her walk and the way she approached the world she was small but boyish. Her nose was large, her chin strong and her brow flat more like those of a junior pugilist than of a young girl. She stood no nonsense either and in the neighbourhood streets her peers of both sexes knew that she was not to be trifled with. The language used in the streets around and by all the people she knew was pithy and pungent. People spoke their minds and obscenities fit to blister paint were used freely with vituperation to match. If she was crossed then she was as ready with her fists and her feet as any lad in avenging insults; she spoke her mind without any subtlety and anyone getting on the wrong side of her would have an experience that would make a marine blench for the richness of the profanity, an expanding store of which she had picked up in the local lanes.

It must not be imagined that the young Sal and her family lived in the direst poverty; compared to many other people around them they did not. She worked twelve hours a day at Saltom Pit tending horses and brought home one shilling and nine pence a week. Her work might best be compared to that of a groom for her duties included mucking out stables, curry-combing horses, greasing tack and replenishing feed and water. Her brother, who was a trainee wagoner earned four shillings and threepence a week, whilst grandfather, Thomas, brought in one pound and five shillings from his work as a driver of the steam powered lift gear at Wellington Pit. The sum total was not munificent, but the family did have enough to eat. They could afford beer, their rent, their food and occasionally garments from one of the slop shops in town. This last did not happen very often, because as with most of their class in town they owned but the one outfit and wore it all the time both working and sleeping. They lasted until the stitching rotted and the garments began to fall apart; even then they could be mended or darned. Many neighbourhood children wore what were in effect rags. The combined income also meant that Mary did not have to work, but could spend her time keeping house, which meant in turn that compared to many of the residences neighbouring, they lived neatly, if not too cleanly. The best time would be when John Steel came back from sea with his pay, because unlike many of his associates Sal's stepfather did not blow his money on drink and the dockside drabs, but brought it home to his family. Why would he do otherwise, for Mary Steel was a pretty woman and one to hurry home to after a long voyage? He did not wish her to work, having an old fashioned sort of view that a man's wage should support his wife. Her place was to make a home; the children were another matter.

By the age of nine Sal had already seen more of life than many adults, because she lived cheek by jowl with some of its raw aspects, things which middle class people would prefer not to see. She had been working at Saltom Pit for a year and had seen people brought up injured in horrible ways, and also how others had accepted this and gone back down to work. One woman in particular was found dead at the bottom of the shaft and for a short while it could not be seen how or why she had died. Then it became clear that she had been standing at the pit bottom and a pebble had fallen straight down the cut-stone lined shaft from the beach above.

Striking her skull with the force of a bullet, it had laid her dead in an instant and no blood was to be seen unless you looked closely at her matted hair and saw the dark entry hole of the stone. Sal had seen the corpse taken up the shaft and laid out by the wagonway before being carried away; nor was this the only dead person she had encountered at the mine, or in the area she lived.

There were children down the pit, some of whom had started at the ages of four or five working as 'trappers' sitting in the dark for hours opening and closing the wooden doors in the tunnels as wagons and sleds came past, so that air would circulate correctly down the mine. Some of these infants would work with their fathers at the coal face, picking up loose coal and placing it into sleds, all for two shillings a week. Mary Steel was determined that her daughter would never work underground, but where the air was clean and without the dust that choked throats and brought on miner's lung. She made Sal swear a great promise that she would never work underground; she never did, but there were plenty of other children and infants who had to. Accidents to these youngsters were common, but there was one particularly tragic case where a pair of brothers had come up from the pit, black from head to foot and had immediately dashed down to the sea and dived in to get clean. The eight year old had been caught by a rip current and swept out to sea; his ten year old brother, hearing his cries for help had tried to save him, but he also was swept away and both were drowned. A fisherman offshore got to them too late and brought their bodies to the beach; Sal knew them both and this was one of the rare occasions on which she was really upset.

There was a moment at Saltom though that marked her out as being very different and it happened in 1842 when she was eleven; that was the year that the government passed a law banning the use of women and children in mines and collieries. Lord Lonsdale's agent, who ran his businesses for him, was Mr John Peile, probably the most feared man in town. Not a large man he was ferociously efficient and completely ruthless in his methods; grizzled sideburns and intimidating grey eyebrows marked him as an old fox, dominant in his area and not to be outdone by anyone. Seeing what was coming he had gradually phased out all women and children by the time the act came into force. At this time Sal was learning to be a wagoner and helped her brother, Thomas, who was already experienced in the work, in order to learn the trade. Thomas did not wish to stay on the wagons though and was waiting for an opportunity to work with steam engines, for he had ambitions about modern equipment and the profession of engineer held great attractions for him.

Out of the shaft of Saltom Pit came large baskets or corves of coal weighing two hundredweight, which had to be lifted onto wagons. The work had been done by women until they had been forced out and the wagoners were expected to help. A side effect of the work was that the women who were able to stick to it grew tremendously strong. Sal and her brother would take a loaded cart from Saltom pithead to the cliff; the wheels of the cart ran along a plateway and into a horizontal tunnel cut deep into the sheer face of the land. At the end of this drift tunnel the corves were unloaded onto a platform and drawn up the shaft of Ravenhill Colliery far up on top of the hill. From there a wagon railway ran along the ridge and down towards the harbour. John Peile arrived at Saltom pithead one fine day and saw Sal Madge heaving a basket of coal in company with a man. Being a person of considerable temper and not one to be brooked, he snapped out at the pit manager.

'I gave a clear instruction that all women and girls were to have their work terminated by the end of last month. What is that lass doing here?'

Men did not like to cross Mr Peile; the agent's face was hard and his eyes were piercing, blue and with a gaze like flint; moreover, if you crossed him you would never work in this town again; everyone knew that. He was not a man to get on the wrong side of, and in this case the manager did not know what to say but spluttered. Peile had no patience with him but called Sal over.

'The government says that girls are not allowed to work down't pits. It's not legal any more. Go to the office, get what's due to you and get thee gone now.'

Peile was taken aback when the ugly girl with the short hair came right back at him.

'I'll not be doing that marra.'

'Oh, and why not?'

The colliery manager hid a covert smile at Peile's surprise; he had never seen anyone answer the agent back.

'Cos I need the wuk. How else will I earn me bait? I have to wuk.'

'Do you like work?' Peile approved of people who liked work.

'Aye I do, especially wi't hosses.'

'But the government says you cannot. It's no longer allowed for women and girls to work down a mine.'

'Well it's a good job I don't work down a mine then isn't it?'

Peile looked at her astonished, but the truth of it could not be denied.

'Aye; you don't do you?'

'Nay I don't. Me Mam made me swear I nivver would.'

'But you go into that tunnel.'

'Yis I tek t'oss in there, but that's not a mine is it?'

Peile was taken aback but admitted, 'Nay. It's not a mine.' Then he began to laugh, the corners of his eyes creased and he guffawed loud.

'You cheeky little bugger. There's not many that can put it over on John Peile, but you're right! It's not a mine; it's a bloody tunnel! Not a single nut of coal is cut in it.'

Still chortling he fished in his waistcoat pocket and pulled out a shilling.

'That's for thy cheek.'

Then he fixed his gaze on her, bending down to look her right in the eyes.

'You'll never be a bobby dazzler, but you'll never want for brass to buy your bread. You have wit. I like that and I like thou well, because you like to graft and that is what this is all about. Life is hard and you have to wuk at it.'

He looked icicles at the manager who was smiling uncertainly and hovering; his tone was imperative and indelible.

'You'll keep this lass employed; she's a good 'un.'

Sal did not recognise it, but this was actually a promise of the sort ordained by Pharaoh, to be engraved on tablets of stone, an imperial command; and it was one that was kept long after John Peile was in his grave.

It was soon after this encounter that Sal was transferred to the top of the cliff. For the next fifty years and more she was employed in loading coal wagons, then leading a horse that pulled the loaded wagon along the railway that led to the top of the Howgill inclined plane. At the top of the plane was a turntable onto which the horse pulled a wagon. The wagon was then attached to a rope and pushed down the slope leading to the harbour; the weight of one full wagon pulled four empty ones up, which arrived at a second turntable. As each was turned it was hitched to a horse and sent back towards Saltom pit.

After Saltom pit shut down in 1848 Sal's journey was longer, down the same railway to Croft pit, in all weathers rain or shine, snow and frost, heat or cold. It made no difference to her for she loved her work. Peile was tickled pink by her and went out of his way to say hello whenever he was inspecting the works. Once he asked her what she liked to do, curious no doubt what such a strange girl felt. Her reply brought his robust approval and respect and he was fond of repeating it in company as an example of the mind of his workers; a habit of his which brought Sal a strong measure of respect in the middle class community in Whitehaven for she was the very model of a hard working labourer who did not complain, but worked to their utmost. This was an image that employers found very appealing.

'I love to see the sweat drip from my brow. It means I'm wukkin hard and that pleases me above all.'

'It pleases me too, no end; owt else thou like?'

'Aye; I like them; pretty things.' Sal nodded towards a bank whereon, it being March, a cloud of daffodils grew.

'There's lots of them up here. Them's me favourites.'

'Thou'rt a good lass; I wish all my workers were like thee.'

Peile was never one to mince his words and on several occasions was know to wax very approving of Sal and sometimes in the very best of company. Naturally he told his employer, 'The best man you've got working for you is Sal Madge. She can outwork any on that wagonway; she doesn't get drunk at her employment, swears like a trooper, finishes any fight that she gets in and turns up every day to do her best. If all your men were like her you'd be twice as rich as you are.'

Lord Lonsdale took due notice and Peile, when he retired, passed on his thoughts to Peter Bourne, the new agent.

As Sal grew older and became an adult, she came across the complications in life associated with sex. As has been implied, she was not very womanly in any conventional sense. The subject of women was one upon which her feelings may best be described as 'mixed.' This was largely because she lived in a community where the lot of womankind was not an enviable one; even less so when they were banned from working in the mines. It consisted, so it appeared, of child bearing, squalling babies and never-ending work in the house. When one of the local women was in childbed the usual practice was not to send for a doctor; they cost money which could be better spent. Any woman who was in labour would be attended by the neighbouring women, and if one of them was a 'cunning woman' who could act as midwife, then so much the better. If not then the older and more experienced mothers were expected to help. This was woman's lot and was not something to be hidden, even from small daughters who were expected to know what it was about. Sal was of working age, and even when small, was taken by her mother to attend on several local births, just to be there and to see and learn. She had seen blood and water, screaming, cursing and, yes, she had seen death in childbed, hardly surprising in an age when about one third of all women died giving birth or shortly after from complications. It was the same with ordinary deaths in the district. In an area with a large percentage of Irish labourers where undertakers were a foreign concept and a luxury not to be afforded, the practice was to lay out the dead and hold a wake where the deceased could be viewed by friends and neighbours who came to pay their farewells. Their coffins would be taken to the cemetery by their friends, carried on the back of a cart and followed by mourners on foot. Since typhus, cholera and other diseases were common, so were dead people and even at her tender years Sal knew how precarious life was; many younger residents of Mount Pleasant did not live past their first birthday.

It was the subject of sex that preyed much on Sal's young mind, though it was a matter to which she was no stranger. There were many animals round the streets in the way of dogs, cats, and livestock in the market, and plenty of rats in the locality; they copulated in the open. Sal worked with horses and had seen the way that stallions went for mares, so she was well used to seeing the act of mating, but her experience was not limited to the animal kingdom. Her own bed was against the wall of their room, but on the other side of the cloth was the bed shared by John and Mary Steel, and when he came home from sea there was no disguising what was happening across the room either by sight or by sound. It is worth pointing out that in that day and age such matter of fact proceedings in married life were far from unusual. Many families lived in one room and a married couple took their comforts as best they could; if the children saw or heard, then so much the better for them as they would know what things were all about. Sal did not appreciate the educational experience offered; in fact it rather annoyed her because it kept her awake; she had work at six in the morning and wanted sleep. However, there was more to it than this; in her young mind there was a growing feeling against what she saw and heard. It must not be thought that this was revulsion or disgust; there was none of that about it. No, it was more of a feeling that such behaviour had nothing to do with her, that she wanted none of it and never would. Young as she was, the matter had not yet crystallised into any definite thought, but there was a vague awareness in her mind that women's lives were lived not as she wished to live hers. There was virtually nothing in the female experience of birth, death, home-making or sexuality that she felt anything in common with. Where this would lead, it was, at her years, too early to predict, but decades later, had she been retrospective, she would have seen where the germs of her future lifestyle were planted.

Thus, Sal saw at an early age that the world was run by men and they held all the cards. They won the bread, made the laws, took their pleasure and left women to cope, and expected, in return for the wage, to be waited on hand and foot; she wanted none of it; men had privilege and she wanted some of that. Of course, it was never a conscious thought that she would take on 'male privilege', but by degrees that is exactly what she did. There was never a single moment where she decided that she would live as a man, but she took upon herself to do things that were reserved for men and because of who she was, and her strength and her connections, no one was inclined to question it; or if they did it was at their peril. Part of the reason she was able to get away with it was down squarely to Isaac Tyson.

Isaac did not think of Sal as a woman; he had grown up with her. He loved her just as she loved him, as a brother. He knew that she was not a brother, but from early days called her 'marra' which in those times was a manly greeting not used by women at all. But it was the occasion of the annual sports of 1846, when Sal was just fifteen, that fixed her in the mind of the town as 'different'. It started as a joke. Every year Whitehaven held a sports day on the big field, an open space up on The Mount where houses had not yet been built. All sorts of activities took place including a game of football similar to what neighbouring Workington did with the "Uppies and Downies". There was tug of war and coconut shies, rifle shooting, gymnastic displays and boxing booths. Isaac, however, had his eyes on the Cumberland wrestling, of which he was fond since he excelled at it. He had an idea which he divulged to Sal just before the sports of that year.

'Sal; I think thou should wrestle me at the sports day.'

'Eh have you gone daft? A woman wrestling? They'd nivver alloo it.'

'Oh, but I think they will. It would be a novelty thing you see. We'd pass the hat and give a cut to the organisers. They'll ga for it for the laugh I think.'

'But you'd beat me easily'

'Nay. I'll let you win. You throw me and the crowd will love it; a lass that throws a man; it'd be the talk of the town.'

'They're not daft; they'll know it's a fix.'

'Well of course they will, but that doesn't matter. They'll laugh like hell and that's what they'll put into the pot for. Ask Mr Harker to pass the hat; they'll not say no to him.'

Sal had agreed of course; it was a good idea. Mr Harker was a rising star at William Pit and hoped to manage it one day, so he was a good man to ask. At the end of the wrestling matches in the afternoon of the games, the organiser of the wrestling had announced a novelty match between a man and a woman, a sight not seen before in the county and probably no other place on earth.

In Cumberland wrestling the opponents stand chest to chest, each locking their hands with their arms round the other's body. Their chin is placed on the right shoulder of the man they hold. When this hold is firm the referee gives the word to begin and the wrestlers commence to grapple with all their strength. The bout ends when any part of a man's body other than his feet touches the ground. If the men fall together then the man who touches the ground first is the loser. The various moves to try to upset an opponent are called 'chips', thus a move to push the opponent off balance by shoving against his shoulder may be called a 'chip on the shoulder'.

Sal and Isaac took off their jackets to much applause and clasped each other in the usual hold. There was not the slightest sense of anything sexual about it and many in the crowd remarked that Sal looked more like a man than a lot of men did, some even avowing that she was a man in a skirt. It is needless to describe the 'match' for it went as planned. Sal 'stood' and Isaac 'fell.' There was a lot of clapping and cheering and Mr Harker's hat passed round full of pennies, halfpennies and farthings. It was what happened next that began the process of Sal becoming a legend. A large collier called Jack Ostle stepped forward.

'I reckon that was a fix. You might have all the appearance of an ugly bloke, Missy, but I reckon I can tip you over easy as owt. I'd put money on it.'

'Easy Sal,' said Isaac. 'Thou don't have to do it. He'll throw you.'

'Will he though?' said Sal. 'How much you got mister?'

'Five bob I throw thou.'

Sal looked in the hat at the money they had collected and did a quick calculation in her head.

'You're on.'

The crowd was interested now. This was not a fix; this was a real match. Their number increased and the interest spread as people pushed closer, craning their necks to see.

'He'll try to lift thee. Thou hest to try nut t'let him.'

'I know it,' said Sal and went forward to form her hold. Sure enough, when the referee gave the word, Ostle tried to lift her, but she was ready for him and chipped sideways, throwing him off balance. He put out a foot to save himself and at that precise moment Sal threw her entire weight into a forward shove that sent him backwards, toppling like a tree onto the ground with her on top of him. The crowd went mad; the lass had shown she could hold her own against a real opponent. There were future games in other years and more matches. Some she won and some she lost, but there was no doubt that from this day forward she was a figure known around town and one held in some respect. There were other reasons why she was held in respect, as we shall see later, but for the moment it is necessary to digress to look at some of the character and life of another of the town's well known citizens as he is instrumental in this tale, but not in a good way. This was because he was a young man, too often drunk, too often loud, obnoxious and up before the magistrates. In short, he was known as a bully, a lout and not a good man to be around. Whitehaven had its fair share of these, but he was a prize specimen.

Chapter 3

An Assault

Saturday night in Whitehaven was always a busy time for the town's police force. Much of the male population was composed of miners, labourers, manual workers and sailors and when the week ended, with the Sabbath morning ahead to sleep it off, many of them wanted drink; a lot of it. As the evening drew on, even on a cold February night, there were large numbers of drunks on the streets, spilling out from the numerous bars, illegal shebeens and public houses. Most of them were harmless enough; the maudlin ones were weepy and grew sentimental, speaking of their mothers, their families or their dearly loved wives at home. Generally all a police constable had to do was clap them on the shoulder and tell them to go home. Most complied; those that did not were the ones who fell over and slumbered in corners. They had to be dealt with; if not then they might be found dead from the cold when daylight came. Drink took different men in different ways; some of the drunks disturbed the peace and they had to be silenced, one way or another. Whitehaven's residential centre was closely populated by prosperous middle class shopkeepers and businessmen who paid their rates and expected their streets to be kept in a civilised state. This meant that sailors singing bawdy songs at the top of their voices or colliers bawling out ballads with leather lungs had to be quiet, or be arrested and taken away in the wagon which patrolled the streets, transporting malefactors to the police cells. This large black carriage with barred windows made a regular sweep of the dockside area because its services were in regular use.

PC Thomas Beattie had not been enjoying his evening, having had more clients than most of his colleagues. One in particular had been violently sick, in itself not unusual, and he was inured to it; this one however had vomited copiously over Beattie's trousers, his shift did not end for another hour and the stink was enough to make a pig blench. As he made his way along the quay, picking his footsteps carefully to avoid the numerous hawsers and ropes leading out to the flotilla of vessels tied up in the wet dock, he had good cause to sing under his breath, "When constabulary duty's to be done, to be done, a policeman's lot is not a happy one." A good man that Mr Gilbert; he understood what it was like to be a copper, and Mr Sullivan's tune was a pretty one too. He had driven his wife daft by singing it all the time since he had first heard it at a variety night in the Oddfellows Hall in Lowther Street. As he turned down the West Strand he heard a voice shouting hoarsely ahead of him and the sound of something being banged quite hard. Just what he needed; the final type of drunk was ahead of him - a violent angry man with too much beer in him, working out his aggression by smashing things. Beattie broke into a trot and there not too far ahead was a man with a hefty wooden batten in his hands setting about a pile of lobster creels, smashing them or trying to; he was not having a lot of luck as the netting and rope round them broke the force of his blows. All the while he was screeching incoherent cries of rage intermingled with common or garden obscenities.

'Oi! Stop that!' yelled Beattie and quickened his pace to stop any more damage being done to property.

The drunk's attention was firmly on the approaching policeman. It was for sure that he had drunk a skinful and he staggered as he squared up to the approaching Beattie.

'Fuck off. Fuck off you fucking bastard or I'll fucking smash your head in with this.'

He was drunk but capable of violence and not drunk enough to render him unable to carry out his threat. Beattie drew his truncheon and as the drunk lunged at him, the policeman rapped him on the hand and made him drop the batten onto the ground. It did not stop him though; as Beattie attempted to grapple him and grab his arms, the drunk kicked hard at his leg and made contact. Beattie recoiled with the pain of a hacked shin and the drunk kicked him on the other leg. Beattie was now in trouble. He recognised the man as Edward Parker, a violent previous offender with no morality whatsoever. He had been arrested on numerous occasions and up before the magistrates as many. He was also large and strong, being a manual labourer. Beattie needed help. He reached quickly into his breast pocket and brought out his whistle. Panting somewhat from exertion he managed to blow the whistle repeatedly. With any luck PC Lewis on the other side of the harbour would hear it; but he was a long way over at the end of his beat and for the moment Beattie was alone. Parker bent over unsteadily and picked up the thick batten again.

'You and me you bloody copper. You and me you piece of shit; not so big are you now Mr bloody Beattie. I fucking hate coppers.'

If you had asked Sal Madge her opinion of herself then she had drunk too much; it was Saturday night though and much of the working population did the same. However, she was not staggering and although her thoughts were rather bleared she was still able to think. With her was John Connelly a friend of hers of long standing. He was in a similar condition to her, but he was a large man and to a casual onlooker he might not have appeared to have been drinking a lot. John was a blacksmith and had been employed at Ramsay's, a marine engineering company, for fourteen years; normally a steady man with a good reputation, he held down a regular job. His only great weakness was the drink, and on some occasions he drank himself into a stupor. Tonight had been comparatively moderate; he and Sal with some pitmen had been playing cards in the Blue Anchor hard by the Mount Steps and had just emerged to make their separate ways home to their beds. A few yards from them Edward Parker advanced towards PC Beattie with the billet of wood in his hand.

'Hey you stop that,' said Sal, rather faintly as she really felt quite sleepy now that the cold air hit her after the stifling warmth of the pub. Parker took no notice of her.

'John. John, that's PC Beattie. He's a good lad. I owe him John. Do me a favour and stop that laal shite will you. I'll see you right.'

'Yis Sal. I'll do that for thee.' The blacksmith lumbered forward.

By this time PC Beattie, seeing his peril, had recovered himself and went for Parker, grabbing his arm and forcing him to drop the piece of wood again. Parker was out of his head and gave an animal like snarl and sank his teeth into PC Beattie's thumb. Poor Beattie yelled out in agony, but now John Connelly arrived. Blacksmiths are strong. He grabbed Parker's hand and forced it down and behind his back. The drunk was surprised enough and let go of his bite on the policeman's hand.

'Who the fuck are you? What are you doing helping this scum? Lemmee go you bastard.'

Connelly took no notice but made to grab Parker's other hand. He did not have to; a patter of heavy footsteps heralded the arrival of PC Lewis who grabbed the drunk's other hand and forced that also behind his back. PC Beattie was able to get out his 'bracelets' and handcuffed Parker.

'Thank you, who ever you are. That was a great help.'

'No problems at all marra,' said the blacksmith through a haze of goodwill to all men. 'I was happy to be of assistance conshtable.'

'I can see you've had a few yourself my friend; no matter; you did good tonight and I'd simply advise you to go home to sleep. Who's that with you?'

Sal Madge stepped out of the shadows.

'Couldn't see thee get hurt now could we, Thomas?'

'You asked this man to help? Well I'm grateful Sal; thank you an'all.'

'I still owe you lad; I didn't help thee mesel, but it's a down payment.'

The drunk had sobered somewhat with the handcuffs on his wrists, but he was still angry and malevolent.

'I know you John Connelly. I know where you live. You're gonna regret this you wanker; I'll pay you back, just see if I don't.'

'Any time marra, any time,' replied the blacksmith, who did not recognise the speaker at all.

'You're paying nowt at the moment you bugger,' said PC Lewis, delivering a round-handed slap to Parker's cheek. 'Carry on like that and I'll find myself forced to knock some sense into you. Right, come along with us.'

PC Beattie had finished tying his handkerchief round his thumb which was bleeding heavily.

'You'll need to see a doctor about that, Thomas,' said Sal.

'Aye I will. I'll see you around Sal.'

The policemen took Parker, one on either side, kicking struggling and spitting towards the quay where they would wait for the police wagon to appear. As the drunk was dragged away he screamed back over his shoulder, 'I'll get you for this Connelly. As God is in heaven I swear I'll get you for this.' As they turned onto the quayside Lewis had had quite enough.

'The hell with this,' he said to the night air, and delivered a punch to Parker's jaw that stunned him to silence.

'Resisting arrest,' he said to Beattie. 'I'm fed up with this bugger; I can't remember how many times we've had him in this last year and he's nowt but a gobby little radge. I'd like nowt better than to knock seven bells out of him, trouble we've had.' Beattie nodded; Parker would be in the cells all day Sunday and would appear before the magistrates on Monday morning. He was a nuisance well known to the Whitehaven police and occasionally in Workington.

Of course a file was circulated to local solicitors who might wish to speak up for Parker, but none did and he certainly could not afford to pay one. Thus it was that he appeared alone in front of Mr Jefferson on the bench at Whitehaven police court the following Monday morning. His day in the cells, the flavourless bread, water, and porridge that they had served him, and his sense of injustice, as well as his normal feelings of rage towards the world made him sullen. To the men on the bench he looked like a resentful recalcitrant lout. They listened to what PCs Beattie and Lewis had to say and noted that Beattie had to be attended by a doctor who put a stitch into his thumb where one of the accused's teeth had penetrated to the bone. Mr Jefferson, who was the chairman of the bench that morning was an employer of men, an importer of spirits and one of the richest and most influential people in town. He did not mince his words when he addressed Parker.

'You are an habitual criminal and drunkard who has appeared in front of me on several occasions. You have been detained in the police cells and you have been fined on each of those occasions. I see no sign that your behaviour evidences any kind of reform and the patience of this community and this court are at an end. It is evident to the members of the bench that you need a salutary lesson. You will be fined fifteen shillings for being drunk and disorderly.'

Parker immediately grinned; the amount was a slice out of his weekly wage, but he could manage it without undue difficulty. Mr Jefferson had not finished though and the rest of his statement took the smile off the culprit's face.

'Not only did you assault a policeman and resist arrest, but you caused injury to an officer and show no remorse whatsoever. Your conduct and your attitude are a disgrace and richly merit an element of punishment from this court. You will serve a month with hard labour in the county gaol in Carlisle. Remove the prisoner.'

No longer smiling Parker was taken down to the cells. A few hours later wearing leg irons and handcuffs, he was taken to Bransty station, an object of ridicule and derision to members of the public; he knew some of the people he saw and his face burned in embarrassment to be seen this way. Illogically, he still blamed John Connelly for his plight, reasoning that if the blacksmith had not pinned his arms he could have made good his escape and gone to another town. Between two policemen, seated on the wooden slatted benches of the guard's van of the train, Parker was taken to Carlisle station. There he was handed over to two warders from the county gaol who were there in response to a telegram sent ahead of the prisoner. It was not long before the large wooden gates of the prison thudded closed behind him and he was ushered into a small room near the gate. Here a grinning warder cut his hair off with a pair of scissors, then lathered his head with shaving soap, prior to shaving it smooth. After this, his scalp bleeding from several nicks and feeling cold, raw and humiliated, he was taken into a tiled white room where he was ordered to strip naked and his clothes were taken away. Then he was given a bar of carbolic soap and told to wash himself as a warder turned a hose on him. This was all part of a humiliating regime designed to make him not wish to reoffend and end up back here again. The cold water stang his skin and the carbolic burned his eyes; he dried himself on a towel that had evidently been used by a lot of people, to judge by its grey appearance. Now shorn, free of lice and fleas, reasonably clean, he was taken straight through to a small single cell with an iron bed, and a window onto the prison courtyard which could be seen only through bars. His first week would be spent in solitary confinement; if he behaved himself he would be put to share with some other inmates. On the bed were a rough grey woollen jacket and an equally rough pair of trousers all marked with the broad black arrow that showed they were the property of Her Majesty's government.

'You'll put those on and then follow me. You've got hard labour and hard labour is what you'll get.'

Parker was too dazed by the shock of finding himself where he was to put up any form of protest. When he put on the prison uniform, the coarse cloth prickling his skin, the warders took him down to the first punishment room. In this chamber there were some crank handles sticking out of the wall and he was instructed to turn one of them. It was stiff and hard to turn. If he slowed down or let up the guard in the room shouted at him to get on with it or he would see him suffer for it. After an hour of straining at the crank, turning it round and round another guard came in and he was allowed to stop.

'Bit of a rest for you; treadmill next. Follow me.'

'What does the crank do?' asked Parker.

The guard slapped him on the face. 'You do not talk. You do not ask questions. You obey. Do not speak unless you are required to speak. Do you understand?'

'Yes.'

'You will call me sir; do you understand?'

'Yes I understand.'

The guard slapped him on the other cheek.

'Yes I understand, sir.'

'On this occasion I shall answer your question as it gives me a certain satisfaction to do so. Your work does nothing. Absolutely nothing. It is utterly useless, just like you. The whole thing is futile and boring and its purpose is to make you work and to break you into obedience. Nothing is gained except your complete obedience and that is what is required of you. If you do not obey there will be consequences. The treadmill also does nothing, but you will walk it for an hour because the law says you will. There is a silent rule here. You do not speak at any time; to me, any other guards, any other prisoners; not nobody. If you do there will be consequences. Now shut your mouth and follow me.'

For the next hour Parker was on the treadmill; a long sort of wheel with steps onto which up to ten prisoners mounted side by side, facing the wall and holding onto a rail while they walked. Their work powered no machinery and neither, contrary to rumour, did it grind corn. It served no purpose except to demoralise with the pointlessness of it all. When this was done, it was time for a meal.

As a prisoner sentenced to a month of hard labour Parker was a class three inmate; as with the other classes, depending on length of sentence, his diet was prescribed by the Home Office and never varied.

His breakfast would be eight ounces of bread and one pint of gruel. Dinner, served in the afternoon, to which he now went was eight ounces of bread, and one pound of potatoes unless there were none to be had in which case two ounces of cheese, for four days a week. On two days a week it would be eight ounces of bread and three ounces of cooked meat without bone. For one day it was eight ounces of bread and one pint of soup. Supper never varied; it was eight ounces of bread and one pint of gruel. Parker was not to have his supper this evening.

After thirty minutes during which time he sat in the prison dining hall in perfect silence, eating his lunch with about forty other prisoners, Parker was ordered back to the crank room. It appeared that the prisoners ate in shifts, which kept them separated into manageable groups. His shoulders and arm muscles were aching and sore; when he got to the room and saw the crank in front of him he snarled, 'I ain't doing that. Do what you bloody well like.'

The warder looked at him fondly and seemed amused.

'Oh I am glad you said that Parker. There is nothing like it for bringing variety and interest into my day. Come along then; I shall put you back into your cell.'

Locked into his cubicle Edward Parker wondered how it had been so simple. All he had to do was to refuse what they said and they put him back into his cell. He was fine with that. The sound of feet came tramping along the corridor outside and four warders entered, followed by a fifth. This was the chief warder, a Crimean veteran who had faced the Russians at Inkerman and the Alma and stood in the thin red line. Watery blue eyes stared at Parker as if he was something the cat had dragged in.

'So, prisoner Parker, you have refused an instruction to work; is that right?'

'Yes sir.'

The chief warder looked at him and nodded, almost as if in commiseration, and then he made a small gesture with his hand. Four warders each took an arm or a leg. Parker was caught by surprise and struggled, yelling and protesting. The chief warder nodded and one of his men sank a fist into Parker's stomach. He doubled up and stopped struggling. They carried him down the corridor, opened a door and took him into a bare cubicle. A few iron ringlets were set in the floor and to these they shackled him by leg irons.

'Two days on bread and water whilst fettered, and then we shall ask you if you wish to work.'

The door clanged shut behind the guards and Parker was left sitting, chained to a bare stone floor. To one side was a metal jug of water and on the other a bucket for necessary functions. As it got dark someone threw a blanket at him and he wrapped it round himself; it was not sufficient to keep out the bone chilling cold of the floor. He lay, sleepless for much of the night and his thoughts centred on the man who had brought him to this; John Connelly. His mind twisted and produced poison for his waking moments and for his dreams. He fantasised about accosting Connelly and smashing his face in with a club; or stabbing him, even beating him in fair fight and humiliating him; but this last made him afraid. He had felt Connelly's strength and did not think he would win. If it had not been for that interfering busybody sticking his nose in to help that copper - a copper for christ's sake! He would have floored the copper; knocked him out and got clear away. The steps up to the Mount were a few yards away; he could have disappeared into that rabbit warren of alleys and corners. He could have followed the mineral wagonway down to Croft Pit and got over the country to Egremont; then south to Barrow where he was not known. He could be working, drinking, seeing girls; and instead he was here, all because of Connelly. Well, Connelly would get what was coming to him, aye and with interest.

After two days on bread and water, chained to the floor they asked Parker if he would work. He said he would, so for the rest of the week he worked the crank and walked the treadmill. When it was over he was mentally and physically exhausted, his brain almost in a trance where life seemed to be nothing but trudging and turning. In the second week some variety was introduced into his regime when he spent part of his day picking oakum. He was given a metal hook and a basket full of lengths of old rope which he had to pick apart using strength and the hook. Oakum at least had a variety of uses, from weaving into mailbag cloth, to caulking the wooden decks of ships.

Prison actually had its pleasant aspects. Once a week every prisoner had to have a warm bath with soap. Parker learned that he liked baths and being clean. If you were not on bread and water the bedding was good and the straw mattress comfortable. The whole building was warm and airy. Those who had not been sentenced to hard labour were able to borrow books from a library; Parker was not given time for that. There was also exercise in a yard. Never a walker Parker was now forced to walk round in complete silence for one hour a day, circling round the space, rain or shine, but breathing fresh air and not the fug of the taverns he frequented every night.

There was a downside of course. At his second meal he sat opposite to a large man who was wolfing down his bread and meat. Parker made the mistake of tearing his bread in two and putting half of it down. To his disbelief the large man opposite took his bread; when Parker tried to get it back he got a huge hairy fist in a violent blow to the side of his head which made him see stars. Now he knew fear and in future kept his bread in one piece and firmly in his hand.

There was another sort of fear. One morning he was not woken at six am as usual but all prisoners were confined to their cells. He heard men taking a prisoner down the corridor and he looked out through the barred door. Behind the group was the chief warder, the prison governor and a priest in full robes carrying a bible and praying. The prisoner at the front was weeping and being almost lifted along by warders on either side. A short time later, just before eight o'clock a voice was heard crying and pleading, shouting that he was innocent and please have mercy. The cries were muffled and then there was a thumping as of a falling weight. Carlisle gallows had claimed the life of another convicted murderer. That night and in the following days Parker dreamed of hanging John Connelly.

After one month of hard labour Parker was released. Having paid the penalty demanded by society for his crime, he was free to return to Whitehaven. He had no wife or family there, but a few acquaintances who thought him quite a man. Now that he had done time in the county gaol he would probably be a hero to them. It was easy enough to get labouring jobs and when his belongings were returned to him, he signed the receipt to find that there was still money in his purse. Heading for Carlisle station, his head showing the unmistakable mark of a released convict, he bought a third class ticket for Whitehaven. His appearance inspired such fear that he considered that it might be an advantage to keep it that way. Once back in Whitehaven though he resumed his old habits. By day he laboured at the coal hurries. By night he gambled and got drunk; every night. He even saw John Connelly and PC Beattie round the streets and did nothing; he had done his time and they had no business with him. At heart he was a coward and a blowhard; for all his furious thoughts about revenge he had neither the courage nor the imagination to carry it through; or so it seemed.

Of all that was in Parker's head, Sal Madge and John Connelly were blissfully unaware. Sal had been in the shadows when Connelly helped with Parker's arrest so he knew nothing of her part in it. For them life went on much as it always did, Connelly at his work and Sal; well Sal had been spending more time with family. One of her regular companions in pubs for pints and cards with a good smoke was Richard Tubman, deputy manager at Wellington Pit who was married to Sal's aunt; a very good and influential connection to have in her line of work. Sal did not know it of course, but old John Peile's instruction that Sal would never want for employment had been passed down through the managerial hierarchy of that pit. It had, after all, been Peile who sunk it; she was not in any danger of having no work and more than most people in the town, she had a job for life.

Sal had never been very close to her brother Thomas who had achieved his ambitions to become winding engineman at Croft Pit. Thoughts of high rewards and marketable skills encouraged him to go further afield, so he and his wife had emigrated to Australia a few years previously; the large coalfields there offered too much promise for him to ignore. There was a significant age gap between Sal and Thomas, for five years can make quite a difference in attitudes, and in her mind the closest thing she had to a brother was Isaac Tyson. There had been uncle William, her father's brother; he had been an engineman at Wellington Pit and later on at Wilkinson's white pottery in the Ginns, but he had emigrated to America in 1869 and no more had been heard of him; presumably he was prospering well in the coal mines of West Virginia. However, Thomas had a son, John Madge, who had been old enough to work for himself when his father decided to try his fortunes in Australia, but he did not wish to go as he was seeing a girl in Parton, and had stayed in Whitehaven. John Madge, like Sal, was a wagoner, but he worked on Howgill Staithe at the bottom of the incline, not on the main wagon way as did Sal. He and his wife Ann had three girls and the first one was called Sarah after Sal, which bound them into Sal Madge's heart for evermore; the others were Ruth and Mary. They lived up at High House in Kells, not too far from where Sal had lodged for so long. Her position in the family was something between grandmother and favourite aunt and although she did not live with them, she was always welcome in the house, her arrival being greeted with squeals of delight. Sal knew that John had turned out well, but would sometimes tease her nephew about marrying a lass from Parton of all places. For a time there had been some development of Parton with a view to turning it into a rival for Whitehaven, but it had eventually failed because of the opposition of the Lowthers.

'There's nothing wrong with coming from Parton Sal,' declared Ann Madge. 'It's a grand spot. It was painted by Mr Turner you know.'

'The artist Mr Turner? He's been gone for a few years now.'

'Yis I know, but he liked Parton. He used to sit there and draw stuff.'

'How do you know? I can't remember, but I think he died before you were born.'

'Aye, but my Nanna saw him, and not only that she talked to him; asked him what he was doing.'

'Why did she do that? It must have been fairly obvious what he was doing; drawing a picture.'

'Aye, but he put boats in it that weren't there and she saw it and asked him why.'

'What did he say?'

'She said that he said, "Artistic license my dear. Even dramatic license!"'

'What does that mean?'

'I don't know; and neither did she so she thought she'd better say nowt and took herself away.'

'So what was he like, this Turner?'

'Nanna said that he didn't look like a famous man at all. He was short and stout with a red face. He had a nice deep voice though and he seemed a jolly sort of man she said.'

'Well it goes to show; no matter who they are, great or small, famous or not, in the end, they're all just folk.'

There was the root of Sal Madge. Unimpressed by rank or money, she treated people in direct relation to the way they treated her. Single and childless, she was nonetheless firmly rooted in her community, her feet like roots drawing strength from the town. It might have been that she felt lonely, for most humans have an inbuilt need to find partnership and intimacy, but it did not show outwardly. She appeared to be content with what she had and liked herself enough to be happy with her lot, for she drew her self respect from her capacity for arduous and difficult work. Her existence was useful, with purpose and she served her town well in a number of ways. Whatever loneliness she may have felt when the door closed on the day, when she took herself to bed at night, was between her and her bedroom wall. She did not want for company either at work or leisure, and had a host of friends and people who respected her. Ugly and grimy she might be, with regrettable hygiene and dirty habits, but she was also as honest as the day was long, hard working, loyal to her friends and as full of integrity as a red squirrel's cheeks full of nuts; she also had a will of steel and the strength to back it up. It is a great pity that Edward Parker, fuming and resentful, plotting an inchoate revenge, did not know this.

Chapter 4

Mr Atter Appears for the Defence

Edward Atter bit into his toast with a degree of animosity on the morning of 7 March 1887. He was feeling out of sorts and for good reason. It was Monday, and the usual session of the Whitehaven police court would be sitting this very morning to rake over the offences that had been committed over the weekend and previously. He knew very well that he should be more philosophical about matters, but he had lost a case the previous Monday which he felt that he should have won and the aftertaste of it still rankled him. His ability to be objective professionally had been severely strained and the sour thought had been turning over and over in his brain that what constituted law did not always equate with justice. He knew this full well anyway; had he been in any doubts about it then old Brockbank would have put him straight with a few terse and pithy phrases to the effect that he must rise above decisions that did not always go the way he would wish or were even unjust. He had not the power to alter them, and even though it might be possible to ameliorate their effects, even that might not be achievable. This had certainly been the case on the previous Monday.

James Murray from Workington, aged 24, had been arrested and arraigned at Whitehaven police court for stealing two pheasants from John Southward, a farmer at High Harrington. The previous Friday morning the farmer had found that his outhouse had been broken into and two live pheasants that he kept in there had been taken. He had reported it to Workington police, though Harrington was within the jurisdiction of Whitehaven's court. PC Scott stated that he had been on patrol in Workington when he saw the prisoner go into a game dealer's shop with a basket. Acting upon a hunch he followed him and asked what he had in the basket. The prisoner had replied 'nothing' and tried to bolt. PC Scott prevented him from running and opened the basket, which he found to contain two pheasants. He taxed the defendant with stealing them and Murray admitted that he had stolen them from a back yard at Harrington. He was then arrested and eventually transferred to

Whitehaven police court cells where he admitted to poaching on Winscale's Road.

Mr Atter appeared in defence of Murray in what was a *prima facie* case of theft. His contention was that the birds were wild and alive and that no larceny had been committed. In other words wild live birds had been placed in the outhouse by the farmer, but being wild they were no more his property than they were of the accused. In addition to this the farmer had identified the birds as his own. How, Mr Atter had asked, could he possibly identify those particular pheasants as his own?

Edward Atter knew very well that Murray was a thief and that his case was hopeless. He had done his best to give the three presiding magistrates some elbow room to be lenient and humane. They had declined the opportunity and sentenced Murray to a fine of thirty shillings or a month in prison with hard labour. Murray had been stealing precisely because he had not enough money. He could not pay the fine so was sent down to Carlisle gaol to graft for a month. As he left the wretched man had wept bitterly, as well he might for his life was ruined. He had a wife with two young children; he would lose his post as a puddler at the Workington Iron and Steel Company and his family would lose their support. Atter's heart smote him and he thought of paying the fine himself, but it had been drummed into him that if he did this for every case he lost then he would very soon have no money himself. The rule in his business was not to do such a thing, but the whole reason why Atter was in court meant that the plight of Murray weighed on his conscience, though it should not, and kept him awake at 3.00am wondering how he could have managed things differently.

Atter was not a native of Whitehaven, but had arrived in the town in 1865 at the age of fifteen from Stamford in Lincolnshire, where his father had been the town clerk for many years. Wishing his son to enter the legal profession after leaving Uffingham school, Mr Atter the elder had secured a position for Edward as an articled clerk with Mr James Brockbank whose premises were at 39 New Lowther Street, Whitehaven. Mr Brockbank was a solicitor of many years standing with a prosperous business catering for a wide range of legal necessities. He was also clerk to the Whitehaven magistrates' court and an excellent person with whom to serve an apprenticeship in law. Edward Atter had been so assiduous in learning his trade that he had passed his examinations with flying colours and by 1870 was a practising solicitor in his own right and a partner in the Brockbank firm. It might be thought at this point that the high flying and able Mr Atter, still only twenty years old might have aspired higher and aim to become a barrister, but he had no desire to do so; there were other things on his mind, and in turn these considerations affected greatly how he was seen in the community.

Edward Atter, by the beginning of 1887, was approaching his thirty-seventh birthday and there still burned within him a great desire to change the world in the best way he could. His wish to excel in law was satisfied and he was recognised as a very able practitioner not only in Whitehaven, but in the assizes in Carlisle where he appeared regularly at the county sessions. In the sorts of cases that featured here he was able to display his incisive logic, his wit and perception in much the same way as any barrister on the august stage of the Old Bailey. He felt no need to climb higher.

In politics he was a Liberal, a great supporter of Mr Gladstone, and very active indeed within the local party organisation. In fact, it was not long since that he had been appointed Liberal agent for the constituency. Here lay the clue to his real nature and his real ambition. It must not be thought that he wished to become a member of Parliament, but his politics tied up with a strong christian belief that a person should strive to leave the world a better place than he found it. Mr Atter's business with banks, shipping companies, sales of property and commercial transactions was very lucrative and the clerks he employed to process his paperwork were very efficient. He therefore had time for political organisation, to sit on the board of the local infirmary and also on that of the local commercial bank. In addition to this, his main outlet, his interest, his hobby, his mission and his obsession was in a singular form of philanthropy. Mr Atter represented the poor in court and he did it *pro bono publico*; the accused paid nothing.

In any town of nineteen thousand people there was going to be a certain amount of crime. This was especially true of Whitehaven where there were a lot of immigrant labourers, many of whom were semi literate or even illiterate. They were also, for the most part, very poor, living in squalor, and as able to afford legal representation as they were to travel to the moon. At every session of the police court the local flotsam and jetsam would be washed up on the bench in front of the magistrates and accused of all sorts of misdemeanours. Drunkenness was common, thefts, assaults, larcenies, batteries, frauds and fratching of all kinds ended in arrest; in front of the bench a stammering culprit might find himself or herself quite unable to defend themselves and end up in prison or worse simply for the want of a decent voice or argument. This was where Edward Atter came in. If the court found that the accused could not afford legal representation they notified Mr Atter at his offices. He in turn would interview the client and decide to represent or not; he preferred to defend rather than accuse. If Mr Atter felt that the case was a deserving one then he gave it his full professional attention and his best abilities. Many a miner or dock labourer facing hard labour and months in Carlisle gaol found himself free because of Edward Atter's eloquence. Sometimes it was convenient for Atter to go into the roughest parts of town to interview witnesses and families; into dens of drink, prostitution and drugs where no law-abiding citizen would venture; yet no one laid a hand on Edward Atter. He received smiles of recognition, respect and touches of the hat and if anyone had dared to threaten him their shrift would have been short but not merry.

Edward Atter, behind his smooth face and fierce moustache was, in many ways, like an ascetic monk in his dedication to his beliefs. To him, law was an instrument of justice and should not be for sale. To be evenhanded and fair, law had to be available to all, no matter how poor or outcast they were. The men and women who made up the very dregs of society were all too often made scapegoats in clearing up cases where the real offenders could not be found. In Mr Atter's view too many men and women had been arrested, held, then sent to prison for long terms, or even hanged with insufficient evidence to establish their guilt beyond doubt. Injustice happened all too often in the magisterial system where the justices of the peace, although their instincts might be commendable, were amateurs, wrestling with a body of law that they all too often did not understand thoroughly. Atter on the other hand lived and breathed law. He was as yet unmarried and his working day did not end with office hours. He did an excellent job for his company, and made Brockbanks a handsome amount of money. In his spare time though he would work later into the night looking at cases where the defendants could not possibly hope to pay a solicitor's fees, and he did it for nothing. Of course he was not unique in this; there was no system of legal aid and decent solicitors up and down the country would work out of a sense of public service, asking nothing more than that justice be made out of law. Atter also prided himself on taking a scientific approach to his cases and he insisted on imposing this in courts where he appeared. More compliant solicitors might not have been so strict, but the local justices were now well used to Mr Atter's demands for evidence; always evidence. Juries and magistrates of course could find people accused of crimes guilty even if there were no evidence; in the end it was down to their opinion, but then again the courts were the haunt of journalists these days and the proceedings in courts were reported often word for word. No magistrate wanted a bad reputation so unlike the old days, evidence had a lot of weight in Whitehaven police court.

On this particular Monday morning Mr Atter was in a rather ambiguous mood. Out of sorts, yes, but determined that this Monday he would do better than he had the previous week.

'Can I get you anything else, Mr Atter?'

'Some more coffee would be very welcome, thank you Mrs McIlwraith. I feel the need of it.'

'You were up late sir. You work far too hard I think; it would be better if you got more sleep.'

'I thrive on it; have no fears on that score.'

'Busy day today sir?'

'Yes; a young man in rather a lot of trouble, but I fancy I can get him out of it.'

'Well if anyone can sir I am sure it will be you. I'll get your coffee.'

Mr Atter was as yet a single man and lodged in the house of Mrs McIlwraith, a respectable widow at number 1 Seaview in Bransty, which was as eponymous as the name suggests for it did indeed have a magnificent outlook over the Solway and out towards the Irish Sea. He had lived here in a pair of rooms for a number of years and found it comfortable and convenient, save for the misses McIlwraith, Mary-Anne and Marion making eyes at him. They looked in vain, however, as Mr Atter was considering changing his circumstances with regard to Miss Cameron, daughter of Mr Peter Cameron, chairman of the Whitehaven Joint Stock Banking Company; a most advantageous match.

Mr Atter was greatly ambitious and had thrown himself into the life of his adopted hometown. Forming an alliance with Mr Robert Jefferson, a member of one of the richest famies in Whitehaven, he had set up the Hound Trailing Association in 1870. The sport had become extremely popular as had Atter along with it. He sponsored the Boy's Foot Racing Association and gave a silver trophy for them to compete annually in their sports. So the up and coming generation looked on Atter as a man of substance and influence; the Atter Cup was coveted. His reputation suffered no harm at all from his involvement in the community and was worth good hard cash when he became the solicitor to go to with business.

When not working or occupying himself in the life of the town Atter liked to go fishing and was often found at the Anglers' Inn at Ennerdale Lake on nice weekends. Atter was personal friends with Lord Lonsdale who had attended the same school as he had, though at a different time, and they had a shared love of horse racing, often attending the Grand National or the Derby together. His large and prominent dark moustache was welcome in just about any great house in the county. A marriage with a respectable lady of some fortune would be the cherry on his social cake and he did not think that Miss Cameron would be against the idea. In fact he rather thought she would be in favour. Let it not be thought that Edward Atter was wholly mercenary in what he did. This would be far from the truth; educated at Uppingham, one of the leading public schools in England, he had been steeped in the tradition of public service and ancient Roman virtues; he was incorruptible, full of ideals and muscular christianity and thought that a civilised man should play a full part in the life of his society.

Such high thoughts were not in his mind at this particular moment though; for now Edward Atter finished his breakfast, put on his coat and top hat, took up his cane and headed out of the door. It was, he was pleased to see, a dry fine day and his walk would be a tonic, not a trudge. He stepped out lively, down the remaining slope of Bransty Hill, past the station, past the Grand Hotel, through the Roman style arch and into Tangier Street, thence to Strand Street exchanging greetings with acquaintances as he went. On his way he passed Sal Madge whom he knew by sight and repute and nodded to her as she to him, both characters well known in the town. Atter noted that she was carrying a bunch of daffodils, and he briefly wondered who they were destined for. When he came to the corner where New Lowther Street began he turned right, crossed the road and entered his offices. They were conveniently placed for business, being almost right next to the docks, the only building between the solicitor's office and the dock railway was a large old warehouse that had been turned into a seamens' mission. Here, for a little while he could give instructions to his clerks, scan through some papers and set a few matters in order before heading up to the police courts where he had to arrive at about 10.00am.

Whitehaven police station stood on Scotch Street next to the town hall. It was an imposing building strongly built in blocks of local stone and joined by an archway to the town hall next door. Through that arch went malefactors and malcontents of all kinds as well as the innocent and the unfortunate, to be confined in the police cells. Fronting into the courtyard was the police court where police officers would arraign men and women who had been arrested in front of a panel of magistrates, usually three or four local men, and detail what crimes they were alleged to have committed. Occasionally, the case would be prosecuted by the person who was supposed to have been the victim of a crime or the solicitor representing them. Mostly it was police officers who prosecuted; the defendant could speak for themselves or they could have a solicitor. That was where Mr Atter came in.

The panel of magistrates this morning consisted of four men, with Mr Henry Jefferson in the chair. Messrs Dickinson, R Jefferson and the Rev Fox completed the tally; all experienced justices of the peace, well used to dealing with local criminality. There were few formalities before the accused, Patrick McArten of Moresby Cottages, was hauled up into the dock. In this case the police were not in charge of the prosecution for the alleged victim of crime had an employer who had engaged a solicitor, Mr JD Fidler of Workington to press her case. The charge was serious for McArten was accused of assault and attempt to ravish a young woman called Sarah Patrickson, a domestic servant in the house of Mr Dixon of Quality Corner, Moresby. Prompted by Mr

Fidler, this young woman described what she said had happened to her at the hands of the accused.

On Thursday 3 March Miss Patrickson went to Whitehaven on business for her mistress. She left Whitehaven about eight o'clock in the evening and reached the lane leading to Quality Street at about half past eight. She noticed a man leaning against a stob (fence post). As she went to pass him he caught her by the jacket and knocked her against the wall. He then threw her down and pressed his knee upon her chest. She struggled and tried to shout, but could not because of his knee crushing her. He then made further attempts to effect his purpose, by fumbling at her clothes, but he heard footsteps approaching, so got up. When he stood up Miss Patrickson scrambled to her feet and ran home to her mistress telling her what had happened.

Mr Atter listened to all this with an impassive face whilst making a few notes in a small notebook. He had already seen the statements which various parties concerned had given to the police. The witness continued with her description of what had happened. The night was clear and moonlit so she could see the prisoner quite clearly. He had on a light grey suit and a black felt hat. She had lived in the Dixon's house for nine or ten months. The prisoner lived at Moresby Cottages and she had seen him frequently. She had a parcel of groceries with her when she was assaulted and left it on the ground when she ran away. Mr Dixon and his sons went to look for it afterwards, but could not find it. The plight of Patrick McArten looked as if it was heading to a foregone conclusion to judge by the face of the magistrates, and the face of the prisoner was a picture of expectant woe. However, Mr Atter's countenance could not be read. He had been informed of the details of the charge against McArten on Saturday, as he asked to be told about any *pro bono* cases that came up. There was no compulsion upon him to take it on. There were very few cases where the guilt was so manifest that he did not waste his time, but decided in each instance that came to him which ones he might succeed in. Atter was a thorough man and there were aspects of him that almost made him a sort of legal monk, so dedicated was he to his profession and the service of justice. After reading the case notes carefully on Saturday, on Sunday after church he had strolled up to Moresby cottages and spoken with McArten's common law wife and her daughter, then to the neighbours. He had a good impression of the man he had to deal with and had decided to take the case. Now he stood up to question this witness.

'How old are you Miss Patrickson?'

'I am eighteen sir.'

'And before working for Mr Dixon you were at the Waverley Hotel. You left there with a good character I believe?'

'Yes sir, I did.'

'Now may I ask, after the assault upon your person were your clothes torn or damaged in any way?'

Her face changed to one with a guarded expression; her employer had seen her come in after the alleged assault so she could not say otherwise than what was true.

'No sir, not torn or disarranged in any way though my hair was pulled down.'

'And you were thrown upon the ground you say with the assailant on top of you, his knee on your chest?'

'Yes sir.'

'Were there any signs of dirt or marks upon your clothes of any kind when you arrived back at Mr Dixon's house?'

The witness hesitated again, a strange expression on her face, 'No sir. When I got home my chest hurt and I felt sick, but there were no marks of dirt upon my clothes.'

'And how long were you struggling with this man upon the ground?'

'I should think about ten minutes sir.'

'I see.' Mr Atter raised his eyebrows and looked towards the bench. 'Thank you; no more questions.'

Mr Fidler then called Mrs Mary Dixon, wife of Mr Dixon of Moorgate, Quality Corner. She attested that it was the girl's night out; she did not have to be back before 9.00pm. She came into the house about nine crying and complaining of feeling sick. She was a girl of good character whom the witness trusted. Her husband went to look for the parcel the girl had left in the road, but it had not been found yet. Mr Atter looked almost bored; he had been checking the witness statements given to the police as to when they were called to attend. He stood to question Mrs Dixon.

'It is my understanding that although Miss Patrickson left a parcel lying in the road, she did bring home two pounds of butter and a shilling's worth of eggs.'

'That is correct, sir.'

'She then told a story of a man having attempted to commit a rape upon her by throwing her to the ground and assaulting her in a violent fashion for about ten minutes.'

'Yes sir.'

'May I ask if any of the eggs were broken?'

Mrs Dixon looked astonished. 'No sir; they were not.'

'Thank you Mrs Dixon.'

The next witness was Jane Wright, the daughter of William Wright, who was the landlord of the Rest and be Thankful Inn at Quality Corner. She stated that the defendant came into the inn at about nine o'clock on the evening in question and he was heavily under the influence of drink, so much so that she had refused to serve him any more. Shortly after this another man came into the bar called Scurr. Mr Atter was satisfied in cross-examination to find that his client was refused drink because he was so drunk that Miss Wright thought he might fall over.

PC McKay stated that he was called by Mr Dixon and interviewed Miss Patrickson who gave a description of the man who had assaulted her. The following day he apprehended Mr McArten and brought the young lady down to see the man at the station. She identified him as her assailant in the constable's presence. Upon this McArten was arrested and charged.

When the prisoner was examined by Mr Fidler he said, 'I never saw the lass in my life and the man who was with me can say the same.'

Mr Atter was forthright in speaking to the bench.

'I must allude to the statement made by baron Huddleston at Warwick assizes to the effect that after eleven years experience as a judge, and a long experience as a barrister, his opinion of cases such as this were that twenty-five percent of them were trumped up stories and it was the men, not the women who needed protection. The probability in my mind is that the story before this court is a trumped up one and a lie from beginning to end.'

As may be imagined this caused a ripple of comment across the court and the magistrates sat up to pay attention.

'The complainant has stated that after struggling for ten minutes on the ground with the man who assaulted her, that there was not so much as a scratch or a stain on her; not the slightest trace of dirt. After being thrown down and running home in an agitated state she did not break a single egg of the shilling's worth she had carried. She did not mention the butter and eggs in her statement to the police, being cunning enough to know that if she had taken those things home without mishap it would look bad for her.'

Mr Atter paused for effect, 'It was also very dark and there are a lot of men who have light grey suits and dark hats. I wish to call Mr William Scurr who has already made a statement about the events of the date in question.'

Scurr was called to the witness box and administered the oath. Mr Atter continued.

'Mr Scurr lives at Moresby Cottages and is acquainted with the prisoner. On Thursday afternoon he met Mr McArten in the market place in Whitehaven and had a glass or two with him. They then went to a pawnbrokers where the prisoner bought a watch which they set going by the market clock. On the way home they called at the Sunny Hill public house. When they reached the quarry at Quality Corner Mr Scurr felt the call of nature and left Mr McArten for a few minutes. He did not hear any disturbance or hear anyone running. After about ten minutes he came out of the quarry to find that the prisoner had gone, and he found him in the Rest and be Thankful Inn. They took out the new watch to admire and look at and it was 8.20pm. Is this a correct version of your recollections Mr Scurr?'

William Scurr said that it was.

'Miss Wright said that Mr McArten came into the bar of the Rest and be Thankful about 9.00pm, though she was not precise. The complainant has stated that she was assaulted in the dark by a man in a light grey suit and dark hat at 8.30pm when my client was in the bar at the inn, a time verified by Mr Scurr by reference to a brand new watch. Since he cannot be in two places at the same time, my client did not assault Miss Patrickson. Although she said she identified him the following day it is simply impossible for it to have been Mr McArten.'

Mr Atter sat down and a discomfited looking Mr Fidler stood up.

'Mr Scurr, what condition were you in?'

'Rather drunkish.'

At this point the court dissolved into laughter. When it subsided the witness continued, 'But I knew what was going on.'

The next witness, Mary Ann Studders, said that the prisoner lived with her at Moresby Cottages and her seventeen year old daughter. He had always behaved himself as a decent and respectable man. When he arrived home on Thursday night there was nothing unusual or agitated about him. Her testimony was hardly necessary; Mr Atter had done his work.

He made a brief closing statement and said that even if the time of the alleged assault were to be left out of the examination, the claim that a young woman could struggle violently with a man whilst lying on the road for ten minutes and come away without a mark, a scratch or a tear, or even a trace of dirt, was absurd. There was a brief consultation on the bench then Mr Jefferson spoke to the court. There was, to his mind, some doubt in regard to the evidence. Consequently, the charge would be dismissed. The prisoner was released and immediately burst into tears of thanks, wringing Mr Atter's hand. The accuser left the court with her employers who were looking thunderous, but where that would lead, Edward Atter neither knew nor cared. Neither did he worry about why she had done it, though he had a theory. It was not unknown for maidservants who got themselves into trouble with their lovers to put themselves into a position where they had been forcibly been got with child; that way not so much stigma attached to their actions. On the contrary, a virtuous girl in trouble because of a vile attack could get a lot of sympathy and help. Edward Atter had no sympathy at all with Miss Patrickson. She had made a spurious charge against a man which was palpably absurd when examined against circumstance and evidence. This was the essence of Mr Atter and the hallmark of his approach. The law was quite clear that someone accused of a crime was innocent until proven guilty. If the evidence did not do this then they must be freed. There was no vainglory to him; he was doing his job and although he worshipped God and was a devout member of the Church of England, he also worshipped justice.

The case being over, Mr Atter returned to his offices to pursue more lucrative matters which provided the money he needed and which allowed him to serve the poor and indigent of Whitehaven without fee. On a whim he walked down Duke Street and turned left when he reached the crowded quayside. He liked the busyness of the place, the grime, the smoke, sailors, fishermen, dockside labourers all provided colour and vitality, which reminded him again of why he had stayed in this town. He loved its industry, its dynamism, and its endless opportunities for a man like him. Hearing a roar in the mid distance he looked up towards the Howgill incline to where a wagon had reached the bottom. It was run up against some buffers at the end of the overhead gantries called "The Hurries" and then tipped so that two Whitehaven tons of coal cascaded down into the hold of the waiting collier underneath. There the trimmers would go at it hammer and tongs with their shovels, spreading it so that the boat was evenly filled. Across the harbour was a forest of masts and spars for there were literally dozens of ships in the port of all shapes and sizes. The busiest part at this particular moment was to the north where was the Queen's dock. This was a wet dock that had been built in 1876 and ships could be moved about round the clock to be filled with coal, iron, gypsum or any other local product to be shipped out by the thousands of tons to places all over the world. Hundreds of men laboured there in what to a casual observer might have looked like chaos, but was in fact ordered, purposeful and very noisy. The rest of the harbour was quiet at the moment as it was tidal and although there were dozens of virtually flat bottomed and shallow draughted craft sitting on the mud, there was little to be done with them until the water floated them again. Still, on many of them men busied themselves with masts, rigging and spars, like so many bees about their tasks. Atter smiled at the familiarity of the scene, filled his nostrils with the salt air over the docks, then turned to go into his offices to earn his daily bread.

Chapter 5

Sal Madge and the Rockets

It must not be imagined that the ability to beat a man in Cumberland wrestling, or fear of her prowess with her fists, or even respect for her love of hard graft were the only reasons why Sal Madge was held in great esteem throughout the town. Respect is a thing which is earned, and there is no doubt that Sal had carved for herself a place in the world of men by dint of sheer hard work. Day after day and six days a week Sal drove her wagons along the mineral railway, filling the job of a skilled driver and she was generally acknowledged to excel at the work, being as good as, and better than most men. The one thing that puzzled any newcomers to the wagonway was her apparel. On a blustery day when the wind blew across the top of the ridge and plucked at clothes so that women found it difficult to make headway against the gale, their skirts acting as sails, one collier was speaking to Isaac Tyson at the pithead of Croft Colliery,

'There she goes; I have to say Isaac that I cannot understand why she's kept to a skirt. I mean look at her; if she's not careful she'll get blown away.'

Isaac laughed.

'I think you'll find when you've been here not much longer why Sal's stuck to her skirt. It's never stopped her doing what she wanted. Do you know I've seen her climbing on the cliffs in it?'

'She never did!'

'Oh aye, she did. It was when we were a lot younger mind. There's some crags and cliffs down towards St Bees just past the old Saltom Pit. She was working on the wagons there and some of the men used to climb for eggs.'

'Seagulls you mean?'

'Yis, and whativver else they could get. Eggs is eggs, whatever bird they come from. Anyway she'd shin up to get her share. I think she still does it when she walks out that way. Flirt likes an egg or two; so does she for that matter, especially when they're free.'

'A bit dangerous dressed like that.'

'I don't think that would stop Sal if she had a mind to do summat. What time do you mek it?'

The collier fished in the pocket of his grimy old waistcoat and grimaced at a battered pocket watch. 'Coming on for eleven.'

'Aye well, Sal likes her tea strong and sweet and she had about a pint of it an hour ago. If I'm any judge just keep watching her until she gets the wagon in the lee of that platelayers' shed. That's a regular spot for her.'

'Spot for what?'

'Haud on a minute; yis, thear she gaas.'

As the watchers observed her from a distance Sal, who cared not a whit, took herself out of the wind, hoicked her skirt up to her knees, leaned slightly forward and pissed in a perfectly straight line down onto the ground.'

'So that's why!'

'Of course. A woman wearing britches would not be able to piss standing up and she'd have to bare her bum. Sal's a wagoner; she has to be able to piss as she goes along wherever necessary, just like a man, does she not? Mystery solved?'

'Aye, I think it is! There's a lot of rumours you know; that she's a Molly or a Maff.'

'I'm not interested in rumours marra. I've known Sal since she was a laal lass and believe me, she is a lass. An unusual one I'll grant you, but a lass nonetheless.'

'There has been some talk that she likes the ladies if you know what I mean.'

'I do know what thou mean, but I would advise thou not to listen to idle gossip. There's not an ounce of proof of that, and even if there were it's not against the law is it?'

'Oh I know that; it's not like it is with men; they can go to prison for a very long time for being a bit queer that way, but for women the law says nowt.'

'You know she's a pal of mine, a marra?'

'Marra is for men.'

'Sal is as a man in most ways, more than a woman at any rate. She's the exception and I repeat, she's a marra.'

'What about Mary Connolly? And Mary Robinson eh? There was talk.'

Isaac Tyson's face set as stone, 'Like I said, there's not an ounce of proof and it's idle tongues that wag about such matters. You'll oblige me by dropping the subject.'

Mary Connolly - there was a name from the past. After the death of her mother in 1852 Sal Madge had lived in the house of Mary Connolly, a widow and a labourer on the coal bank. She worked with Sal and her job was to tip coal into wagons. It was a congenial arrangement for two friends who worked closely together and it lasted a few years. Lives were often shortened by fever, typhoid and cholera in this district of Whitehaven and so it was with Mrs Connolly. Seeking new lodgings Sal heard of a room in the house of Mary Robinson another widow, but young and pretty with three children. Mary scraped a living by setting up a small shop in her front room, but three children were a lot of mouths to feed and the rent from a single female lodger was welcome. People are people though, and it was not long before a few tongues began to wag to the effect that Sal was acting as Mary's husband; whatever that meant. It was Isaac Tyson who raised the matter with her; he was the only one with guts enough to do so. They were sitting near the slipway *scoppin a feuw styans in't watter.*

'You know they're talking about you and Mary don't you?'

'Who is?' replied Sal in a disinterested way throwing another stone.

'Folk around, you know.'

'I don't knaw and I don't care.'

Isaac came straight out with it.

'They're saying you're her man Sal.'

Sal thought on this matter for a moment whilst chewing her quid.

'Well that can't be can it, for I am not a man.'

Then she laughed loud, finding the idea very funny.

'You live like one Sal; who's to say you don't act like one? Are you one of those women who love other women? You take her flowers don't you? I've seen you go home with them.'

Sal looked at Isaac with a peculiar expression on her face.

'What if I were? Would it mek any difference to thee?'

'Not to me, Sal. Who someone beds is none of my business. But it might to some.'

'I cannot see why it should for the life of me. I take daffodils home when they're in season, for I pick them along the line and I like them.'

'Well there's many as might see it as unnatural and that you're taking flowers home for thy lass.'

Sal Madge began to laugh, then to laugh some more; she laughed until the tears rolled down her cheeks creating lines in the grime.

'Unnatural! Unnatural! Tek a look about thee marra!' She gestured with her pipe towards the smoking chimneys, the railway lines, the cramped squalid houses.

'You think it's natural to live this way? Eh? Is smoking natural? Is filling yer kite with beer, staggering home barely fit to stand and punching thee wife if there's no food ready natural? Are steam engines natural? Or tunnelling miles out to sea burrowing in the earth like rabbits for coal; is that natural?'

She spat a gob of brown spittle onto the floor to emphasize her derision at the thought, 'We mek this place the way we do; there's nowt natural to it.'

'Look Sal, I agree with thee, but there's a lot of small minded men round here who accept you as thou are, but if they saw you as another man and in competition for lasses, then they might think different. Things could get a bit hot for thee.'

Sal looked at him thoughtfully. 'I like it hot,' she said. 'But I'll tell thee summat. If there's any as try to mek it hot for me, I'll mek it a damn sight hotter for them. You know I would.'

Isaac stopped and looked at her, 'Yis; I know you would. Just be careful.'

'Look Isaac. Don't you ga fretting aboot me. There's not yan amang them can see through brick walls, whativver is garn on in my lodgings. They can tattle all they like.'

'Is it true?'

'Now that's what they call idle curiosity marra and I'm surprised at you asking.' Her eyes crinkled with amusement though and her shoulders shook a little with repressed laughter.

'That's for me to know and you to find out; but you never will and neither will they. It's none of thy business nor anyone else's.'

That was as frank a discussion on the subject of Sal's love-life as anyone ever got, so the matter must be regarded as a closed book. However, there is one grace note, outside the scope of this work. Later in her life, after Sal had been living above Mary Robinson's shop for some years, Sal was sitting smoking her pipe by the fire one evening when the youngest daughter asked her a question.

'Are you my Daddy?'

The corners of Sal's weather-beaten face creased into a wry smile and she thought that Mary must have a word with Ellie about the facts of life.

'No my pet, I'm not thy daddy.'

It was Mary Robinson whose eyes were troubled when she overheard this question. She had heard the rumours that Sal was her 'husband' and found the gossip hard to take; next day she told Sal this. Sal would not be a trouble to anyone. That very hour she arranged a swap of lodgings with another wagoner, an elderly man who needed more looking after than she did. She moved into number 5 Windmill, up at Kells, way above Mount Pleasant and close to the wagon railway. It was a short walk across the fields to reach her workplace from there. Whatever other result this move may have had, it stilled the wagging tongues and Sal found herself rooming in with a numerous family of Kennedys of all ages and close to some relatives of hers, John and Ann Madge at number 9. Another wagoner who worked with her was John Kennedy at number 8 with his wife Bridget and their three children. Although Sal was much older than them, this was another house where she was welcome, and John was a particular friend. She lived surrounded by Catholics and she was not of their faith, but it did not bother her a whit. In a town deeply divided between Catholics and Protestants, one with an Orange Lodge, she took no sides and discriminated between them in no way at all, having no time for intolerance. Her view was that she did not care what people were so long as they treated her squarely, and if they did that then they got it in return.

Sal was right in her assumption that idle gossip could not harm her. She lived in a town where heroes were common; men of the sea, men of the mines, labourers; all lived in dangerous work environments where perils of all kinds threatened constantly. In mine rescues, in saving of life at sea, in industrial disaster ordinary men of the town showed their courage and their heroism was often blazoned across the local newspapers. There was, however, one woman who was a heroine; she might be working class; she might be ugly and dirty and smelly, but the courage of Sal Madge was never in doubt and it crystallised in her work for the Rocket Brigade.

Rockets as military weapons had been introduced into Britain in 1804 by Sir William Congreve, who had observed their use in the Mahratta wars in India. His first rockets were almost as deadly to their users as to the enemy, being highly inaccurate and liable to come back and blow up the people who sent them off. Gradually, however, they had become more reliable and the British Army used them as a standard weapon until 1850, when an improved design by a Mr William Hale had made them spin and become highly accurate. It was not too long before it was realised that rockets had potential to save life at sea, or more accurately, from the sea. Most ships were sail driven and at the mercy of the wind. Very often ships were wrecked simply by being driven into shore and in weather that all too often was too dangerous to launch a lifeboat. A rocket carrying a thin line could be fired out to the stricken vessel and the crew would be able to haul a rope from the shore to the ship and make it fast. It was then possible to physically pull survivors from the sea who would otherwise drown. The idea caught the imagination of the public, especially in those who used the sea for their trade. The Whitehaven Volunteer Rocket Brigade was set up in 1848 and it was not long before Sal Madge joined it. At first she was not wanted, but she was a crack wagon driver and that was what they needed. All the other wagoners appeared to have families or other things to do, the Rocket Brigade being a voluntary organisation with no pay. Her professional reputation in what she did stood high, and so she was taken into the Brigade, not as an enlisted member, but as a civilian wagoner. No doubt the idea was to replace her with a suitable man at some point in the future, but that moment never came; Sal was superb with horses and the doyenne of drivers. The desire to replace her faded into history as if it had never been and soon the brigade were proud of their unique driver and would boast of being the only outfit they knew that had a lass for a driver; and she was good mind, damned good.

The rocket house was situated on the north pier of Whitehaven Harbour near to the lighthouse at the end, and in this low building were kept the six rocket firing racks with all the equipment necessary to take them to where they were needed. It was heavy stuff and needed a wagon of some size to pull it, with a team of four large horses. The brigade held a meeting and a dummy rocket firing every month; from the word 'Action' they took a mere twelve minutes to set up the equipment and fire their rockets. The volunteers wore uniform with caps and were under discipline, commanded by Captain Dixon with Lieutenants Boyd and Harris all ex Royal Navy. Sal, as wagoner, did not have to wear the uniform, but turned up in her own clothes and drove the horses at a canny lick to where they needed to be. The excitement of these occasions appealed to her and she could crack a whip as good as anybody, so was a valuable member of the team. During its existence the rocket brigade had attended numerous shipwrecks and had saved lives.

At eight o'clock in the morning of Tuesday 26 October 1875 Sal was at the top of the Howgill Incline waiting for a return wagon to go back to Croft Pit when down below in the town a gun went off. Immediately after the report another gun shot a gout of white smoke over the north harbour. It was quickly blown away by a very strong wind that was bringing rain in off the sea. This firing would be repeated in five minutes; the Rocket Brigade was being called to action.

The Brigade possessed two small cannon; if an alarm came in and the company had to assemble then these guns were fired, the noise being heard all over the town. Sal had fifteen minutes to reach the rocket house or things would happen whether she was there or not; best that she was, since none of the others were much good with horses. Within two minutes she had informed the foreman at the top of the incline and was pounding down the cobbles at a trot; soon she was crossing the busy quay, people getting out of the way for they knew her mission, and saw other figures running towards where the equipment was stored.

As she roused out the horses and harnessed them to the large brigade wagon, Sal heard Captain Dixon shouting out details of the emergency,

'There's a ship gone ashore at Barnscar; it's stuck fast, the sea is breaking over it and the crew have taken to the rigging.'

'Where's Barnscar?'

'It's down by Seascale, Sal.'

'That's a bit of a run.'

'Don't be daft; I've had a train put on.'

Sure enough Sal drove the tall wagon at a smart pace, loaded with men and equipment up to Preston Street station where the station master had arranged for a flat bed truck to be hitched to a shunting engine which was all ready to go; there were lives to be saved and Whitehaven's rocket men were up for it.

'All traffic's been stopped on the down road; you've a clear run.'

By 9.30am, one and a half hours after receiving the alarm, the train pulled into Seascale station. It was immediately obvious how dangerous the plight of the sailors was, because huge waves were pounding up the shallow beach with enormous force as the tide came in. The ship was aground and stuck firmly on the rocks, but with the water approaching full tide, she was far out of range of the rockets. The only hope for the crew of the stricken ship was the Seascale lifeboat a brand new vessel named the William Tomlinson, only operational since June, and it now became apparent that only five of the lifeboat crew had turned out and one of them was the coxswain. Eight more men were needed and the rocket brigade did not hesitate; among them was Sal Madge.

'You can't go Sal; you're a woman.'

'What's that got to do wi' owt thou great gowk? You garn to put me out? Now that I'd like to see! I can pull this thing as well as you, sonny boy.'

There was no time to argue and to tell the truth Sal's appearance when seated in the lifeboat was such that any who saw it would have sworn that the crew consisted of twelve intrepid men and the cox'n. The inhabitants of Seascale had turned out in force and dozens of willing hands launched the boat and shoved her out through the rough surf as far as they dare down the shallow beach, until the undertow was taking the feet from under them. The wreck was six hundred yards offshore, firmly stuck on a submerged reef or outcrop, and all the crowd could do was watch anxiously as the boat fought its way through the waves, its oars rising like wings on either side as the cox'n called the stroke. Against the wind they made very little progress and they bent their backs into it, sweating and straining to advance at all. It took them a full hour to gain an offing, so that they could approach the men clinging to the rigging. The lifeboat went past the wreck out towards the sea and then began to allow the waves to carry them down towards the masts where they stuck out from the water. She turned out to be the 'Isabella' - a small and very old wood-built schooner of 53 tons from Port Carlisle, loaded with 86 tons of slates for roofing and enamelled chimney pieces; a heavy cargo. She had been launched in 1825, but was a seaworthy vessel despite her age. The lifeboat backed down delicately and slowly, every yard being controlled by the ceaseless oar strokes of her tiring crew, towards where the ship's company of three men were clinging to the rigging and the watchers on shore cheered mightily as they were carefully brought down into the lifeboat. Captain Roberts of the Isabella was near to fainting with cold and fatigue, having clung to the rigging for ten hours; his two men were in no better case. Both were younger than the captain, but John Owens and Owen Thomas had to be helped delicately into the boat, for they were so stiff they could barely move and their hands were grasped like claws round the ropes of the rigging.

Sal was sweating a lot, which she liked because physical effort was a joy to her, as was holding her own in this situation. Along with the rest of the crew, the wind now behind them, she now braced herself to take the boat inshore to where many willing hands waded out to take hold of it as the keel touched the sand. The crew leaped out as the helpers hauled the lifeboat up onto the wheeled cradle which had been pushed down into the water. From there she could be pulled up onto the beach by the combined efforts of some horses and spectators. There was a lot of excitement and cheering centred around the rescued crew who were being escorted up to the coastguard station to be revived with strong tea heavily laced with rum. Sal climbed out of the boat with no notice being taken of her; thus no account of what she had done appeared in the newspapers, which merely reported that the crew had been rescued by the Seascale lifeboat. She did not care; it did not bother her a jot; what excited her more than anything else was that this was the furthest distance she had ever been from Whitehaven. The brigade members knew what she had done and patted her on the back in congratulations, or even shook her hand, man to man. Sal Madge had done the unusual once more, but then again she was Sal and she almost defined unusual. Word spread around the district and added to her legend and to her status as almost a symbol of the town. Her strength, her honour, her straight talking and yes, her manly habits were a source of pride. She may be smelly, but so were most people; she may never change her clothes; but that was also true of most people. She may not wash so much that the locals had a saying that something was 'as black as Sal Madge', but it was said with a sort of civic delight. How many towns could boast a character like Sal Madge? Not many, and that was for certain.

As an aside it is worth recording that neither the master nor the mate of the Isabella had any form of certificate. The subsequent inquiry into the loss found that despite the weather the ship need not have been lost; the wreck was occasioned by her being taken much too far inshore; the loss was down to the Captain and mate who should be strongly censured for their negligence. As to the Isabella, the beach at Seascale goes out at such a shallow angle that she was left grounded at low tide. In the week following the wreck, her owner, Mr Irving of Carlisle, had the cargo recovered and placed onto a train at Drigg from whence it was taken to its intended destination at Maryport. The ship itself had been insured for £200, but when the cargo was cleared he sold the hull for £46 to a Seascale man to recover what he could.

Sal heard some of this through the grapevine in the days following the wreck, but to her it was incidental. She had joined the Rocket Brigade partly because the romance of it appealed to her; the horses, the dashing to the rescue. It was a manly thing to do and she delighted in such; she had shown her quality, and above all, she had saved life. In this her true nature shone through; under the hard and battle-inured exterior beat a heart that cared about right and wrong, life and death, good and bad; and she was prepared to do something about it. It did not matter what she was, man or woman; to those around her she was admirable, and she did good in her community; that was all that really mattered.

One of the reasons for Sal's popularity among her fellows was that she had an excellent memory and possessed a great store of tales to do with the town. The changes she had seen in her lifetime were so rapid and so many as to almost beggar belief. The Mount, the Ginns and the harbour area might be warrens of poverty and sweated labour, but the centre of the town was what gave away the level of its prosperity. It was beautiful, with well-proportioned streets, a square worthy of Italy, gracious mansions and shops crammed full of goods for sale to people in the locality who had enough money to buy. There were plenty of those. Of course, much of this was due to the business acumen of various lords Lonsdale, or more accurately, to their agents. Coal was king and money poured in from all over the world. Whitehaven did not just depend on the sea, however, for Henry Lowther, third Earl of Lonsdale, had a good friendship with a very great man indeed. George Stephenson was a frequent and welcome visitor to Whitehaven castle and with his experience it was quite impossible for him not to point out the advantages that a railway would bring to the town. Despite the fact that the railway boom had gone into slump and panic because of the swindling activities of George Hudson, Lord Lowther was not put off. The first ground for the new railway was cut at Preston Street in Newtown and over the next thirty years or so Cumberland acquired an extensive rail network.

Stephenson himself was seen around the town a lot, and it was on one of his excursions that he met Sal Madge, on whom he made quite an impression. The story of the meeting was one she was fond of telling. She was leading a very large horse called 'Lofty' along the wagonway towards the top of the incline, pulling a well-loaded cart, when she saw a man watching her.

'That's a canny load you've got there,' he said.

Sal looked at him and liked him on sight. A man in his fifties, she thought his face fine, lined with care and with an expression of great thoughtfulness. More than that, she was taken by his accent, which she knew was pure Geordie. Though it was the other side of the Pennines, she was not snobbish about such things so answered him civilly enough.

'Aye, but he's up to it, at least on rails. I will not let them owwerload my hosses.'

'You like hosses then?'

'I do. Doesn't everyone?'

'Well there's some as say that the hoss has had its day, and that locomotives are going to take over from them soon.'

'That'll be a day I would not want to see,' said Sal. 'I reckon the hosses will see me out and I'll be content with that.'

Stephenson looked at her shrewdly. 'I never thought to see a lass doing what you're doing. Being straight with you, that's why I spoke to you.'

'I thought as much; I'm not a lass anyhow.'

'Are you not? Well if you're a man, why are you in a skirt? I took you for a lass because of it. I'll allow that you do look like a man, but did not care to say it for I did not wish to insult you.'

'Well that's where you're wrong,' declared Sal. 'I'm not a lass but a woman full grown!'

'Are you so? I see your point so, I'll tender my apologies for any wrong impression.'

'Oh, you're not the first,' said Sal, 'and I doubt you'll be the last.'

'Tell me then; do you find this work hard?'

'No. Not at all. I love the work and being out here and the company of pitmen and wagoners. Salt of the earth they are.'

'Aye, you're not wrong there, as I well know,' said Stephenson.

Sal eyed his well-made clothes. She had thought him a gentleman, but his voice indicated otherwise. 'You do?' she said in some surprise.

'Yes. I started as a brakeman at a coalmine, not unlike that chap in the hut over there.' Stephenson indicated at the brakeman's hut at the top of the incline.

'Well you look as if you've come up a bit in the world. What do you do now?'

'I'm an engineer. I build locomotives. You might have heard of one of them; it's called the Rocket. George Stephenson's my name.'

He proffered his hand.

Sal pondered for a minute, then shook it.

'I can't say that I have. Sorry marra, but I don't read papers or owt.'

Stephenson laughed, 'Nay there's nowt better for any vanity that might creep up on me than meeting someone who's never heard of me or my Rocket. Alright, tell me summat; what's the gauge of your wagonway.'

'Four foot, eight inches,' replied Sal without hesitation.

'I can see you know your business,' nodded Stephenson approvingly. 'Do you know why it is that measurement?'

'Nay I don't.'

'It's because I used it on the railways I built at Killingworth and other spots. That measurement's been used all over the north of England.'

Sal was far more impressed with this than she had been about the Rocket.

'Why did you choose that gauge?'

'Ah now, it was something to do with the Romans. I could tell you, but it'd take a while.'

'Nay; don't bother. From what I heard they were a murdering bunch of savages,' replied Sal, expressing a profound disinterest.

Stephenson stared at her and laughed.

'Oh dear; all those fine ladies and gentlemen who throw their classical quotes at me and think I talk funny. I'd love to see their faces if I said that to them. Parliament's going to change the gauge anyway to four foot, eight and one half inches. It'll cost a bomb to convert the railways, but they're all daft the whole set of them.'

'Well from what I've seen, most of them know a lot about nowt anyway,' said Sal. 'What are thou doing up here on't brow? Thinking of putting one of thy locomotives here?'

'Nay, marra. I'll leave this one to your horses; just professional interest is all. I am going to build a railway in Whitehaven but not here; rest easy.'

'I'm glad to hear that.'

'Aye well for this sort of job horses are still cheaper than locomotives. It looks like rain's coming on. I'll be about my business for I do not like a soaking. Good day to you.'

Stephenson did not offer to tip Sal and that was a good thing. In later years when she knew more about the man she had met she was fond of recalling how they parted.

'We shook hands, man to man as equals, and he set off back down the steps. No side on that one I can tell you.'

Man to man as equals.

No one contradicted her. They would not dare; this was Sal Madge.

Chapter 6

Drink and the Devil

Perhaps the single greatest problem that a human being faces is also his or her greatest blessing; they have the capacity to think. That said, there are some who think a lot more than others, and on a wider range of topics. The average tenant of Rosemary Lane did not think a lot about matters of life and death, largely because they had other things on their mind such as the roof caving in whilst they were working on a coal face four miles out under the sea, or perhaps wondering if they would escape death or serious injury on their next voyage across the Atlantic or to Australia. The surroundings they lived in did not help much either for there was not a lot of rosemary to Rosemary Lane; quite the reverse, for it was a narrow cobbled way that led steeply upwards from the mill and foundry in Albion Street towards the top of The Mount. It was crowded and dirty; its cobbles never quiet, being a thoroughfare for all sorts of wagons, goods and people. Most of the houses were occupied by numerous tenants, it not being uncommon to find whole families living in one room. The houses clung precariously to the side of the hill and had probably been placed there originally because the land was deemed unusable and therefore cheap. As with the Mount Pleasant and Newhouse areas, it was plagued with fever, dirt and squalor. John Connelly and his family lived there.

Connelly was an Irishman and Catholic, having come over as a young man of twenty-two with his wife Maggie who was twenty-three and their small son Patrick. They had escaped rural poverty in southern Ireland, but had avoided the obvious route for John to take, which was to the industrial city of Belfast. John was a blacksmith by trade and had heard that Catholic craftsmen who wished to work in the factories and shipyards of Ulster could expect to take home half the wage that a Protestant would receive. On the other hand, there was a shortage of skilled labour on the British mainland and he could expect to receive the going rate. Whitehaven had beckoned, and there they had made their way. Connelly had no trouble finding work in the repair yard of the Whitehaven Shipbuilding Company, which operated on the site of the famous old Brocklebank shipyard. Unfortunately, in 1879 the price of iron on the world market soared to such levels that the company found it had to overspend on completing contracts it had already undertaken. They never had a lot of capital in reserve and were forced into voluntary liquidation. John Connelly found himself briefly out of work. This situation did not last long, as he was a steady craftsman with a good reputation for being skilful at what he did; soon he was employed again as a blacksmith at Ramsay's engineering works situated in Albion Street, running uphill from Swingpump Lane. There he made boilers, but graduated to more skilled work, mounting engines in ships and workplaces and helping with other contracts that the firm took on. The company had a foundry within its precincts that made wheels, cogs and gears, beams for engines and all kinds of cast iron mouldings to order. Out of the cast iron they also beat wrought iron; so there was plenty for Connelly to do. He was in a position to do well, renting a house for himself, Maggie, his son Patrick and his daughter Mary-Anne in Swingpump Lane right near work. Then Maggie died at the age of thirty-three. She came down with a fever which the doctor said was typhoid; there was a large number of cases in the town at the time. The infirmary in Howgill Street was full so Mrs Connelly had been placed into the new fever hospital at Bransty, but she did not get better; there had been nothing to be done for her and she passed away quickly. John Connelly was left with two children, a job that took twelve hours out of each day and no one at home to look after things. The boy Patrick was fifteen and out at work; feeling himself a man he no longer lived at home. The girl was only four years old when her mother died in 1881 and had to be looked after, which at first was not too difficult. There were plenty of women living locally who would take in a girl child during the working day for a small consideration. Although Connelly knew that it was not the best thing for a growing girl, there was not a lot else he could do, having no family in the town. Eventually, when she was older, better arrangements would have to be made, but that was for the future.

Men are fragile and brittle creatures, and in Connelly's case this was as true as with any; perhaps part of his tragedy was that it was also true of many women. Maggie's death hit Connelly hard and like so many men in his situation, he sought escape and solace. There are many ways of doing this and Whitehaven could offer most of them; whores, cards, drink, opium, fighting, violence, or crime in many forms; you could take your pick. Connelly's was perhaps too predictable; he found oblivion and comfort in beer. His favourite place to drink his beer was the Dusty Miller just round the corner from work where they sold a dark ale made at the Tower Brewery just up the road at Corkickle. It was good beer and if anyone had told him that it was 7% alcohol he would not have cared. Five or six pints would put him into a state where he forgot all his woes and actually began to feel benevolent towards the world. More than that, and he would not think much at all about anything and relied on his friends to get him home. To his credit it must be said that he restricted his drinking to the nights and was never the worse for wear at work where his stock still stood high and no-one thought the worse of him for liking his beer. Work in the foundry was hot and tiring, the hours long; it was natural that a man should want beer at the end of his day. Beer was regarded as food to a working man, and an extension of his meals; it was almost a right. It is true that many men overdid this and it was a common sight to see children outside the pubs shouting for their father to come home because they were hungry, whilst he spent the wages on beer. The difference between these men and Connelly was that he could afford his habit.

Connelly was fundamentally a decent man who had gone to pieces for a good reason; he was lucky in his choice of pub, for it led to his choice of friends. The Dusty Miller was one of the haunts frequented by Sal Madge and her acquaintances; apparently all good men. John Kennedy was a collier and a neighbour of Sal. Isaac Tyson had risen to be an under manager at Wellington Pit, in charge of the engines which pumped the air for the whole colliery. Sal was known across the whole town and respected; they all liked beer, tobacco both smoked and chewed, and above all they liked cards. Catholic in their tastes, they spread their custom around several public houses in the neighbourhood of the harbour in a regular pattern and in these establishments their business was valued, not just as regular customers, but as a stabilising force. Whitehaven was a place where pub fights were as common as bed-bugs, but you did not start any trouble, as all knew, in any bar containing Sal Madge. She liked a nice peaceful evening and if you started anything you could be sure that she would finish it. It was a conversation over cards in one of these bars in 1883 that led to the next phase of Connelly's life.

'Who's looking after thee lass John?'

'Mary-Anne? Ah, she's with Mrs Carruthers.'

'She's cracking on a bit; and Mary-Anne's seven now isn't she?'

'She is that; and growing like you wouldn't believe. Why do you ask Sal?'

'Oh, just that Elsie Carruthers must be seventy if she's a day. A lass like Mary-Anne must tire her out a bit.'

'Aye well, I pay her to sit in; not much, but it's enough for her.'

'She might be better with someone younger. More energy you see.'

'That's true enough, but I don't know any younger lasses who'd do it.'

'But I do. There's a few I know would be glad to sit in with thee girl; she needs younger company John. It can't be very interesting for her. Different generations you know; there's a time coming when she'll need to be told stuff; Elsie won't do that you know. A younger lass will.'

'Do you have anyone in mind?'

'I do. Her name's Rose Anne Alderson. She's about twenty-one or twenty-two and has just lost her position on account of her employers moving to Carlisle. She did not want to go with them and needs to earn a bit while she finds another place. Not a lot going at the moment. Would thou like to meet her?'

'Is she a Catholic?'

'Yes she is; I know thee mind on that and would not have mentioned her else.'

'I'll have a look at her. Do you want to bring her round?'

'I'll try to bring her to your spot tomorrow.'

Sal Madge did not know the girl particularly well, but she was a mine of information about what was going on in the working class districts of Whitehaven, and so it was she knew of this girl.

Rose Anne turned out to be an able enough companion for Mary-Anne and although not beautiful in any way she had even features, nice hair and enough household skills to make herself an attractive proposition. It was true that Connelly was a lot older than her and a few heads were shaken when it was known that he had asked her to marry him so quickly after meeting her, and been accepted. By and large the community was in sympathy with him though; he was a hard-working man and he obviously needed a woman to perform the functions of a wife in all ways. Death was commonplace enough, so most people shrugged their shoulders and got on with their lives. The problem with the marriage turned out not to be so much its occurrence, as the age gap between husband and wife. It was not long before the patina of the ceremony wore off and they found they had little in common. After four years of marriage he was forty-one years old and she was twenty-six, and there was an estrangement between them; Connelly spent little time at home.

At work he was more respected and this had spread throughout the mining community as he was involved in the contract awarded to Ramsay's Engineering works to test the weighing gear at Wellington Pit. As one of the workmen detailed to carry out the tests, he had been a witness to the staggering fact that the machines were under-weighing. To realise the enormity of the situation one has to reflect that miners were paid for how much coal they cut. This was placed into wagons and a tally placed on each wagon signifying who had cut it. This wagon was then weighed and the men paid according to the weight of coal. On the 20cwt machine the weight being shown was 8lbs under the real amount, for each wagon. When all the wagons of a day were added up then Lord Lonsdale was not paying for a lot of coal. It was John Connelly who suggested weighing the wagons without coal, for the weight of these had been taken as a given. Quite shockingly these turned out to weigh more than 26 pounds over their registered weight. Together with the original mistake, every wagon load was being under-weighed by 34 pounds; his lordship was getting a substantial amount of free coal every single shift. The whole matter was settled by the miners' leaders behind closed doors at the Queen's Head. No lump sums were given, but the means' wages went up slightly. John Connelly received his share of the approbation that came the way of Ramsay Engineering. His reputation was high and it was felt that he would rise within the company. True he drank a lot; everyone knew that, but he was typical of the men in the town.

Outside work it was different; Connelly was out drinking every night. Most of the time he could make it home, if a little unsteadily.

When he had too much he had to be taken home, sometimes carried. He was not an angry drunk; when in his cups he was a sad figure, staring into space and not really seeing what was going on around him. He might respond if shouted at, but it was best just to sit or lie him down and eventually he would go off to sleep and wake none the worse, apparently. The term clinical depression was unknown to him, but he lived a nightmare of grief, dissatisfaction with life and yearnings for something better that weighed on him physically like a great lump in his head. The drink made life bearable. So did work, for he knew he was good at it, but the two did not mix which was just as well for his employers would not have employed the man he was at night. It might have been thought that with a new young wife he would have mended his ways, but he did not like his home all that much especially after Patrick had left and gone to work on the railways. The only thing he and his wife had in common was sex, but he was not too keen on that either because he and Rose Anne no longer liked each other. When sexual relations took place, which was infrequently, it was more as an instinctual thing because they were married, and always under the influence of drink, rather than because of actual love. On Connelly's part he might just as well have been consorting with one of the local prostitutes. Rose Anne had also taken to drink after suffering two miscarriages, but not to beer; her favoured way to oblivion was moonshine gin, which was very cheap. She had always liked a drink herself, which was no bar to the relationship, but since her marriage she drank for another reason and that was Mary-Anne. Connelly's daughter did not like her stepmother. She had accepted her quickly enough as a baby sitter, but then Rose Anne had committed the ultimate crime of marrying her father. To Mary-Anne no one could replace her mother; once the marriage was done and Rose Anne was in Connelly's bed, the jealousy set in. Mary-Anne was now eleven and old enough to be a handful. There were screaming rows between Rose Anne and Mary-Anne.

'You're not my mother!'
'I married your father and that makes me your new mother.'
'You'll never be my mother and you can't take her place!'
'I'm your father's wife.'
'I don't care what you think. You'll not be telling me what to do.'

'I'm your stepmother and you will do as I tell you.'

'See what I mean? You're not my mother and I will not do as you tell me; I do as I want.'

Rose Anne had slapped her, but Mary-Anne took after her father in size and was big in build; she slapped her stepmother back. Thus, there was a declared war between them where Mary-Anne, robbed of her mother by typhoid, would not accept any other woman in the house to take Maggie's place; there was nothing Rose Anne could do. She did appeal to Connelly on several occasions, but he more or less shrugged and told her not to be daft and let a laal lass boss her about. It was women's business; he brought home the wages that paid the rent, provided the food and everything else and did not wish to be bothered with such matters; it was up to her. This was cowardice on his part, a fact he vaguely knew in the back of his mind, for he was well aware he should have imposed his rule upon the household right from the beginning. Rose Anne was a newcomer and the person causing the friction was his daughter. He might have made it clear that he was not going to tolerate this behaviour towards his wife, but he did not; it was easier to do nothing. So he remained silent while the woman he had married tried gamely to cope with her instant family and he said nothing as she started to sink under the weight. If anything, he blamed Rose Anne for what he saw as her failure, though a small voice occasionally whispered to him that it was actually his fault. Mary-Anne knew this of course, that her father could not be bothered and so made it her business to make Rose Anne's life hellish; she was an indulged child who could do no wrong in her father's eyes, so she subjected her stepmother to a corrosive stream of vileness. She treated the older woman with contempt, spoke to her insolently and refused to be of any help whatsoever round the house. Doing the woman's work was what Rose Anne had signed up to so in the washing, the housework, making of fires, cooking and so on, the girl did nothing, refusing adamantly to lift a finger to help. When Connelly was present Mary-Anne was all sweetness and light. When he was not she was snide, nasty, unhelpful and obvious in her dislike of her stepmother.

Connelly's home life deteriorated; he would come home to a badly cooked dinner, if it was done at all. The house became unclean, untidy and the washing not done. What should have been the reasonable dwelling of a better class artisan became an uncared for hovel as Rose Anne took more and more to drink to dull the pain of an existence that was becoming intolerable. Connelly did tax her with neglect of her household duties, but got in return tears and appeals to him to do something about his daughter; he never did. Rose Anne felt more and more like a skivvy whose existence counted for nothing. After four years of marriage it was more common for him to come home and find her drunk than not. She was often unconscious from gin, an object of scorn and pity among some of the neighbours, but the subject of envy for others; perpetual drunkenness was by no means unusual in Mount Pleasant, Newhouses and the areas around. When Rose Anne had drunk enough gin, she was to all intents and purposes dead to the world and could not be roused by anything. If she had been given ether for an operation it could scarcely have had a more profound effect.

That Connelly had a drinking problem was well evidenced by an incident that took place late one night in Swingpump Lane in the Newtown area of Whitehaven. It was a cold night and dark; not many people were about. Connelly had taken six pints of strong dark ale on board and was feeling that pleasant muzzy sensation where life really did not look bad. Shuddering a little with cold he had left the Duke of York where he had been keeping company with some colliers, and was heading towards The Manx Arms to meet some cronies. This part of the town was on the edge of the lit area for the gas lamps did not extend into the streets of The Mount. There had been talk of bringing the new fangled electric street lighting to Whitehaven, but it had not yet happened. A few of the old oil lamps that had lit the town since the eighteenth century still lingered on the Mount, the Ginns and Newtown, but their effect on the surrounding gloom was negligible.

Feeling the call of nature Connelly crossed to the dark side of the street, unbuttoned his flies and began to relieve himself against a wall. As he did so something caught his eye that moved on the road, coming towards him. Hastily he made himself decent and turned to see what it was. Along the middle of the road a huge black dog loped, sniffing, snorting and growling balefully. Its eyes seemed as big as saucers and soon it came level with the place where he stood, pressing himself in horror into the brickwork which refused to give way behind him. Momentarily the dog paused in its pacing and looked right at him as his blood ran cold with fear. Its gaze was diabolical and he began to shudder, his teeth chattering and not just from the bone biting cold. For a breathtaking moment the huge dog halted in the road and, sniffing towards him; his heart almost stopped as it set one paw in his direction, but it did not come any further than that. It appeared to lose interest in him and continued on its way down towards the harbour, disappearing into the darkness. As it turned the corner it looked back towards him and emitted a terrible howl.

Connelly was drunk, and of course people who are drunk enough sometimes see things which are not there. So it was that he staggered rather than walked to the Manx Arms and wobbled his way to the table where Sal Madge was sitting with Isaac Tyson, John Kennedy and a few others. As ever they were pleased to see him.

'Asser Marra? Grab a pew.'

Connelly did not have the local accent so took no notice of the greeting, and drink deepened his brogue as he quavered out in terror, 'I've seen it; I've seen it!'

'Oh aye; what have you seen?'

'The Newtown boggle; I've seen it Isaac, just now heading for the harbour.'

'The Newtown boggle,' said Sal Madge. 'Just how many have you had tonight John?'

'Only a few Sal; I'm not drunk I swear. I saw it plain as I see you now. Like a fiend straight from the devil.'

'So how many hest thou had?'

'Only about six; not many.'

'Six pints. Sit down you daft bugger and shut thy mouth. Best you stay quiet, folk are looking at you already.'

Sal Madge was not one for messing with boggles; she did not believe in them and that was flat. Matters metaphysical were things she had no time for at all; she did not go to church, did not consult priests, whether Catholic or Protestant and her attitude to tales of such was hard nosed. John Connelly was drunk and that was that. She had had a couple of pints herself or she might have reflected that in her acquaintance with Connelly he had never at any time expressed any sort of belief in God, ghosts or boggles; nominally a Catholic, he did not attend church or worship any god that she knew of. He was not in any condition to take part in the games of cards and sat in a corner of the group muttering to himself in a great fear. The Newtown boggle was a portent of things to come, so local legend went. If there was about to be a disaster down the mine; if a ship was going to sink, so the tales said, then the boggle, an evil spirit, would appear in the form of a large black dog; a hellhound. Reports of its appearing dated back for many years and it regularly featured in the pages of the Cumbrian newspapers when people claimed to have seen it.

Connelly's friends dismissed what he said as the product of beer and an over active imagination. When the morning came, so did he; the sun was high in the sky, the day was bright and things of the night were easily dismissed as the result of having a bit too much on a stomach that had not eaten enough. He had managed to get himself home and to bed where he found Rose Anne catatonic from her own drinking. The very best that may be said of John Connelly was that he was a good man at bottom, good at his job, but at life he was sinking into a morass of despair, drink and if he were not careful, an early death for which, if truth were known, he would probably not be sorry.

Chapter 7

A Policeman's Lot

Superintendent Edward Thornburrow was, for the most part, a happy man at the beginning of 1887. He had at last managed to live down any shadow of censure that might have attached to his actions in the Cleator Moor Riot of 1884 and had been awarded a mark of signal favour. The chief constable of Cumberland had named him as a deputy for Whitehaven and district, which meant that his powers were expanded widely; in the case of civil disturbance he did not have to refer to higher authority before he took measures to deal with a situation. He could send for reinforcements, call in the army and take command in whatever emergency may arise and be regarded as acting in the chief constable's name. This was trust indeed and a delegation of great powers, a sign of favour; but it had not always been the case.

Thornburrow was a good copper; he had joined the Carlisle force in 1863 as a constable, after leaving the army. Seen as a good, steady and reliable man, he had worked his way up to sergeant based in Orton, then to inspector at Cockermouth and had been fortunate enough to land a superintendent's job at Whitehaven when the post became vacant. There were two superintendents in the police station; Mr Taylor oversaw the operations of the beat officers, the sergeants and the inspectors. Thornburrow saw to the prosecutions to make sure that the work of the police was not in vain. In through the gates of the station courtyard came a steady stream of drunks, petty larcenists, burglars, rapists, whores, men of violence, disturbers of the peace and so on in a never-ending variety. On arrival, the desk sergeant booked them in and then they were clapped up in the white tiled cells beneath the station. The local magistrates met in the upstairs police court sitting on a bench of three or four. One by one the accused who had been arrested the day before were brought before them. Thornburrow's job was to prosecute them, in person, and fulfilling the task that many might see best done by a prosecuting attorney. He did require a fair amount of legal knowledge, which he had, but sometimes he did not have to. A wronged person, a victim of crime, could if they wished, prosecute the case themselves, and on occasions they hired a solicitor to do it for them. This tended to happen where the victim was seeking restitution or compensation but most of the time it was the job of Superintendent Thornburrow. He had to detail what crime had been committed, describe the conduct of the accused, to assemble witnesses and present evidence enough to get a conviction. Much of his work was simple enough and drunks were told off, and fined, or given a week in the cells. Other cases were deemed by the magistrates to be too serious for the police courts and were packed off to Carlisle to be tried at the quarterly assizes. Thornburrow liked things to go smoothly, but it did not always happen that way. There were solicitors who would give of their time to defend men and women who were the dregs of society and who very often got them off scot free. They would insist on 'evidence' and bandied words around like '*habeas corpus*' or '*Magna Carta*' and 'The Bill of Rights' and so on; they really were the bane of Thornburrow's life. There were people walking round Whitehaven who were as guilty as sin and by rights should have been banged up with hard labour; the superintendent had a gut feeling that they were guilty and his gut never lied.

There was only one blemish on his long career and that was Cleator Moor; he did not see it as such, but he knew that many people felt that his actions on 12 July 1884 were not what they had a right to expect of the police. Thank goodness that the government did not see things that way and the Home Secretary had even defended police actions in the House of Commons. It all began when the West Cumbrian Orange lodges had decided to hold their big rally for that year in Cleator Moor. John Bawden, the leader of the Orangemen in Cumbria had told Thornburrow that he intended to do this thing and the superintendent had asked him if it was wise. Would it not be best for the Orangemen to have their march through a more congenial place like Whitehaven? Cleator had a very large Irish Catholic population and Thornburrow could see that there could be trouble.

'Mr Bawden, you know there could be trouble?'

'I don't see why there should be. All we are going to do is march from the station through the town to Wathbrow, have our meeting then march back. We have a perfect right to do so.'

'Nobody would deny your rights Mr Bawden, but you know how things are in Cleator; nobody better.'

'I should do; I live there and we have a flourishing lodge there too - my own.'

'I know where you live, but with such a large number of Catholics living there, do you not think they might see it as a provocative act?'

'I should think not. This is England Mr Thornburrow. As a freeborn Englishman I have a right to walk where I like that is not private land. The road running through my town is a public thoroughfare. Are you saying I cannot walk down it for fear of Catholics?'

Thornburrow did not know what to say, so he said the obvious; 'Of course not Mr Bawden; you have that right.'

'Yes I do; and if I want to invite representatives of the organisation which I have the honour to lead in this county over to my town, then I have a right to do that as well.'

'Yes sir, you do,' said Thornburrow wearily.

'And if anyone causes any trouble Superintendent, I expect our police to deal with it.'

'I will do my best, sir.'

Thornburrow had indeed done his best, but he had not thought outside the box. A special train had brought over one thousand Orangemen to Cleator Moor on 12 July and they paraded through a town of nearly eleven thousand people, four thousand of whom were Irish Catholics. The situation was like a powder keg and into this Superintendents Thornburrow and Taylor placed themselves and forty-five constables, all they had available. It was hopelessly inadequate, but it was all he could scrape in the district. In retrospect he might have asked for reinforcements to be brought in from other forces; he might even have asked for troops, but he did not. As he had predicted, there was trouble.

The first part of the day went well enough; the Orangemen marched through the town with their fifes and drums, carrying their regalia and playing tunes in commemoration of the Battle of the Boyne in 1690. Huge banners with 'Good King Billy' on them were marched through rows of houses where Irish miners lived; and there was no trouble. Thornburrow had felt greatly relieved when the last of the marchers disappeared down the long street towards the open space at Wath Brow. He and his men were able to relax for a while whilst speeches went ahead and the Orangemen had their services and party.

On the way back all hell broke loose when the local Catholic population came out of their houses and some children began to throw stones at the Orangemen. There followed something that resembled a battle as the Orangemen set about the Catholics with ceremonial swords, pikes and regalia such as maces and chains. People were cut about and stabbed. Thornburrow ordered his men to draw their batons and in the market place they managed to part the two groups. The respite was brief for as the Orangemen continued their parade down towards the station the stone throwing started again. It was then that things got very confused. Thornburrow saw two men run across a field by the Montreal Institute and they pulled revolvers out of their pockets, opening fire on the Orangemen. The Orangemen also produced guns, though who pulled them first was never established. The Orangemen fanned out, firing at the crowd and the men in the field as their parade retreated towards the station. Thornburrow had then ordered the issuing of swords to his forty-five constables and the sight of policemen with these in their hands quelled some of the disturbances. The Orangemen continued firing at the Catholics from their train windows even as it pulled out of the station; all in all one man was killed and about fifty other people had been injured. How many of the sword slashes were inflicted by the police in the course of their duties, no one thought to ask.

When the riot was over Superintendents Thornburrow and Taylor had come in for some criticism for not foreseeing what was going to happen, and not having enough men on hand. This was stifled when Sir William Harcourt, the Home Secretary, gave his opinion that the men Thornburrow had on hand were quite sufficient for the purpose and he could not see why the Catholics had attacked the Protestants. Thornburrow had been smarting up to this time, feeling that his honourable if undistinguished career might be coming to an end, but after Harcourt's intervention his spirits soared.

Shortly after the Cleator riots had brought the actions of Whitehaven police to national prominence, another incident had taken place, which had again put the superintendent onto a far larger stage than he was used to. On 30 August 1884 a charge of dynamite had been placed against the front of some premises in Cleator that belonged to Mr Thomas Moffat, a mine owner; the front of the building had been badly damaged in the ensuing explosion. Of course it was a matter of national news and police reaction had to be prompt. Thinking that it might be a continuation of the Fenian dynamite outrages that had been taking place for several years, Thornburrow threw his energies into finding the culprits. It was a credible hunch that there were Fenian sympathisers among the Irish miners in Cleator who might have carried out the outrage. Upon questioning Mr Moffat as to anyone who might bear him a grudge, the mine owner had supplied the name of Patrick France. This man was a known troublemaker and malcontent; not a good influence in his workplace and given to violence. The matter that finally prompted Mr Moffat to discharge him had been when France got into a quarrel with another miner called Milburn, and he had threatened to kill his opponent. France was used to the handling of dynamite. That was quite good enough for Thornburrow; motive and means were both present and he arrested France; the moment he saw him he knew that he had his man; he had the look. France was brought up before the Whitehaven magistrates on Monday 15 September; he was prosecuted by Superintendent Sempill, Mr Taylor having now retired. Mr Dunne, chief constable of Cumberland was present in the court, but of course the prisoner had to have a defence. Mr Edward Atter appeared to speak for France. Mr Sempill had stated immediately that France had only been apprehended the previous Friday and that not sufficient time had passed for him to be able to assemble his case; he asked for a remand for a week to allow this to happen. He then called superintendent Thornburrow to the stand and the policeman had said quite emphatically that he had reason to suspect that the prisoner was connected with the bombing and evidence would be forthcoming. As he said this he saw a small grim smile cross Edward Atter's face. Thornburrow knew very well the reason for this smile; he did not like Atter. In Thornburrow's mind Atter was like the judge in *Trial by Jury* who sang "And many a burglar I've restored to his friends and his relations." Grudgingly he allowed that Atter did not fit the first part of Gilbert and Sullivan's description of a sharp lawyer, "All thieves who could my fees afford relied on my orations," for he was aware that

Atter worked *pro bono*. The superintendent knew very well that France was a villain, yet here was Atter wanting the man set free. The solicitor stood up to speak.

'I think some evidence ought to be given. The prisoner was taken at Cleator Moor on Friday morning and a court was sitting there on that day. I think it is a remarkable thing that he should have been brought here when a court was sitting at Cleator Moor that morning. No evidence has been given to justify his arrest. On behalf of the accused I say it is not right that he should be detained on the supposition that something may turn up. They ought to give some evidence to justify their conduct.'

Mr Atter gestured towards the police bench. It was the clerk of the court who responded, 'It is the practice in these cases. They cannot all at once obtain the evidence, and if a responsible officer pledges his oath that evidence will be forthcoming, that is enough. In the dynamite case at Birmingham the men were remanded from week to week.'

Atter replied, 'But in that case they had evidence.'

The chief constable was pursing his lips and Thornburrow found himself sweating, but thankfully the court did not see things Atter's way. France was remanded for a week without bail and his case was referred to the director of public prosecutions. At the end of that week France was now being prosecuted by a solicitor, Mr Lumb having been directed to do so. Lumb said that he was not prepared to go fully into the evidence, but introduced two witnesses; Mr Moffat whose house had been bombed, and Inspector Anderson who had arrested France. Thornburrow flinched as he remembered how Atter had taken them apart with his forensic examination; they had not a shred of evidence to offer, despite Thornburrow's assurances of the previous week. The bench conferred and decided that they had to remand the prisoner for another week; Mr Atter made some remarks on the subject of *habeas corpus*, stating that no one should be arrested and held without trial on the basis of no evidence at all. He asked that his client be allowed bail, because all that he had heard against him was hearsay, but this was refused.

The following week Mr Lumb made out as strong a *prima facie* case against Patrick France that could be made, but Atter simply demolished the witnesses and exposed all the so-called evidence as circumstantial, which it certainly was. Mr Atter called no witnesses of his own, but contented himself with pointing out that not a single piece of actual evidence linked his client to the crime. The bench decided to refer the case again to the director of public prosecutions to see if he wished to proceed with the prosecution. To Thornburrow's embarrassment they remanded the prisoner for another week and he still had not produced any evidence sufficient to convict him or even send him for trial. Patrick France had already been in gaol for over two weeks. After this third week he was sent for trial at Carlisle assizes.

All these proceedings were reported in the national press and as may be imagined Thornburrow worked the candle at both ends trying to find evidence to link France to the crime. Already there were discontented whispers in the community that an innocent man had now been three weeks in gaol with nothing to keep him there. The superintendent's spirits had fallen to rock-bottom on Monday 27 October when the judges at Carlisle heard the case until 11.15pm; the jury were out less than five minutes and came back with a 'Not Guilty' verdict. Thornburrow had not made his case, his oath had not made good, and his professional word was not borne out by events. A case in which the chief constable had taken such a keen and personal interest had ended with egg on the superintendent's face; an innocent man had been in prison for nearly a month and had been most decidedly acquitted. The clear implication was that the person or persons who had exploded a bomb at Cleator Moor were still out there and had not been caught; they had got away with it scot free; Thornburrow knew in his marrow that France was the culprit, but could not prove it.

Thornburrow thought of himself as an old-fashioned sort of copper and he knew what he now needed; a high profile case that would restore his reputation as a good law man and a thief taker. He was of high rank in his chosen profession and coming towards the end of his career. Somewhat unimaginative, if he dreamed of anything it was of a sensational crime, or a rich robbery that he could investigate to a triumphant end. That would be the cherry on his cake, the icing on his dreams. The thought of something like the Thames torso murders, or the Pinchin Street torso murder made his professional mouth water. As for the Tottenham Court Road and Bedford Square mystery where bits of people were being found wrapped up in parcels; Thornburrow lusted after such a thing to get his teeth into.

To be sure, by January 1887 it no longer seemed to matter. The Cumberland Police Committee had expressed its appreciation of his long service and he had been entrusted with powers appertaining to the post of chief constable. The committee had stated that they applauded his efficiency and energy in carrying out some very onerous duties. He possessed the confidence and esteem of the public and his colleagues in the police force. These were laurels and of that he was in no doubt for they were balm to his soul, but for the same reason as men climb high mountains or explore remote deserts Thornburrow wanted something to gild the lily of his professional life. The trouble was that cases like that in Whitehaven, crimes which hit the national headlines, were few and far between. Five years from retirement the chances that one would come his way seemed remote.

Chapter 8

A School Refuser

It was a shame that John Connelly was not paying too much attention to the upbringing of his daughter Mary-Anne; this was not solely because of his wilful neglect of the way his daughter treated his wife, but also because he failed to spot the obvious signs that she was unhappy at going to school. When she was very young, Sal Madge's stepfather, to his great credit, did notice his stepdaughter and resolved to take her in hand; Sal did not go to school for when she was a child there was not money for such a thing. Nonetheless, she could read, write and do her numbers well enough, having been taught by her mother. John Steel was far more concerned with another aspect of young Sal's education; he was a sailor and made his living before the mast in as tough a profession as could be found. A man unable to hold his own in the forecastle of a ship would find his life made miserable, for not all human beings are sweetness and light. He was fond of his stepdaughter and worried about her future. His decision to do something about it was taken during a long voyage and he put it into action as soon as he got back. It was just as well that in true Cumbrian fashion the family were all straight talkers, for many a girl would have burst into tears at what he said to Sal.

'Sally if I tell the truth you're no oil painting are you?'

Twelve year old Sal just looked at him, wondering what was coming next.

'I mean to say that you's been dealt a good set of cards, but in the looks department thou's nivver going to be a lass that turns heads.'

'That's true, but I don't want to turn heads.'

'Well you say that now, but you's only twelve. Give it a couple of years and you might think different.'

'I don't think so; I like boys well enough, but not in that way.'

'Aye well, that's what I mean. You look like a lad and you act like a lad. Now to me that means you's got to be able to fight like a lad.'

'But I can fight; I can beat most of the kids round here.'

'I know you can Sal, but when I say fight, I mean a different thing to what thou mean. What you gets up to is not fighting; it's scrapping.'

'What's the difference?'

Steel looked at her intently, 'I've seen you go in with feet and hands thrashing all about the place and I'm not surprised you win some of thy fights Sal, but you's a strong lass and if you did things proper then I think you'd win them all. There's a science to it you see.'

'A science?'

'Aye; you see most people think they know how to fight; to defend themselves, but actually they don't.'

Seeing Sal's evident interest, he continued, 'You see Sally there are places where you can really hurt people if you hit them there. And there's bits you can grab, things you can twist. Then there's different types of punches and blows. You can use feet or fists or elbows; even your head. If you know what you're doing, you can beat the hell out of someone and not get hurt thissen.'

'Can you teach me how to do those?'

'I can and I will for it's a savage world out there my lass and I want you to be able to make your way in it without fear or weakness. But there's one more thing I have not said.'

'What's that?'

'What is in thy head.'

'My head?'

'Aye; most people don't want to hit; a lot of men who are soldiers don't want to kill; but there's a few who do. Hitting a bag of straw is something that they can do, but if it comes to hitting a person most people hold back. They don't have the instinct to do harm; they hold back and that is their weakness.'

'Can you teach me that as well?'

'No. Only you can do that. But if thou ever come up against a big strong bloke who starts trouble because he doesn't like the way thou look, remember two things. Firstly he does not know how to fight most likely, but thou dost. Secondly, he does not want to give it his all because with most people fear of retaliation makes their mind freeze. Get over that and cultivate in thy own head that you art willing to hit and to hurt and you'll probably beat him. I'm not saying that you should start trouble, but if you try to put thissen into that sort of mind then you should be able to finish it.'

Sal had learned to fight in ways that might have been seen in forecastles, sailors' bars, brothels, shebeens, saloons and gambling dens in ports all over the world. But she also took Steel's advice and if trouble started in which she was involved she did not hesitate to finish it in whatever way was necessary.

No such conversation took place between John Connelly and Mary-Anne. The blacksmith was big and strong, but he did not know how to fight, so had no lessons to impart. If he had, then much trouble and tragedy might have been avoided. Mary-Anne was not happy at school. The school itself was not the problem, though it may have seemed that way to later observers; she went to St Begh's, a Roman Catholic school on a site between Chapel Lane and Catherine Street. There had been talk of extending St Begh's across its site to Duke Street, because it was by far the biggest school in town. They provided a good Catholic education to the children of Whitehaven's burgeoning Irish immigrant population; it was adequate, but of a limited range, as the teaching was done by nuns and there was not a single certificated teacher among them. Since the 1870 Education Act the local school committee had oversight of the school, but their funding came from the Catholic Church, so although suggestions had been made that St Begh's might get some trained teachers, as yet none had been employed. In reality, this was of no great importance; children were taught to read, to write and how to do their figures; they were also taught their religion, catechism, creed and prayers so with this came morality. Let it not be thought that this was done in a dry way for it would be an injustice to think it. Discipline was, of course strict and enforced by the sisters with a willow switch if necessary. Its use, however, was not common as any disciplinary problems would be dealt with by informing Father Murphy who would speak to the boy or girl offending. If they did not repent of their ways he would sally forth and speak to their parents; and punishment took place at home.

Pupils were of course required to be clean, but this had become a lot easier for them since 1852, when piped water had at last been brought to all parts of the town, supplying the best that Lake Ennerdale could give. People no longer had to walk three quarters of a mile with buckets and wait in queues at one of the eleven decent wells that supplied over 18,000 people. For the inhabitants of Mount Pleasant the nearest water supply had been on Quay Street, half a mile away; no wonder dirt and squalor prevailed. With water laid on in the streets there was a great improvement with personal hygiene and also the state of the houses. Of course this did not prevent the great outbreak of enteric typhoid that came in 1862 and carried off dozens of people, but it did at least convince the harbour and town trustees to do something about having sewers and drains dug. During the 1860s, as these came into being, Whitehaven became a far cleaner and very presentable looking place, so there really was no excuse for personal slovenliness, at least on Sundays. Cleanliness was next to godliness and if you turned up to St Begh's with a dirty neck or an unwashed face then there would be ructions with the very clean nuns.

The Sisters of St Paul had arrived in Whitehaven in 1870 and their purpose was education; at first they had been a novel sight in the town in their black gowns and broad white coifs, but now they were an accepted part of the scenery as hundreds of the local inhabitants had passed through their classrooms. Under the stern eye of their first mother superior, Mother Aloysius Bowen, they also visited the sick and distressed, doing what they could to alleviate the effects of the direst poverty in their community.

St Begh's was actually great fun at first for Mary-Anne; her best friend was a young lady with blue eyes and blonde hair called Kathleen Hegarty. Together they were the centre of a small coterie of friends who skipped, played, gossiped and went around together. Certain it is that worldly relationships are transient things and apt to blow away in the wind. In any gathering of human beings there are those who like to be seen as taking the lead; a dominant feature that many people recognise in themselves and struggle to repress. Kathleen Hegarty, just like Mary-Anne, had fair colouring and eyes of sea blue; there the resemblance ended for although Kathleen was pretty enough she was large and big boned, whilst Mary-Anne, though sturdy and by no means small, was beautiful. The seeds of destruction were always in their relationship.

The catalyst for the change in Mary-Anne's circumstances was late in coming; she started school at six years old, but children of that age are not always coherent in their likes and dislikes. They learn to hate and bear grudges as they grow into them. St Begh's was famous for several things in the district. The first was the willingness of the nuns to engage in extra-curricular activities, so their pupils were taken on picnics to St Bees, put on an annual show whose quality was much admired, went on nature walks, and took part in parades on certain saints' days. Disaster struck Mary-Anne when she was ten and it fell at Christmas of 1886 when Sister Thomas Aquinas chose her to act the part of Mary in the nativity play. This was a highly coveted role among all the girls in the school and was usually reserved for the most angelic looking amongst them; Mary-Anne, despite her treatment of her stepmother at home, certainly looked the part. Had she possessed eyes in the back of her head and seen the face of Kathleen Hegarty when the parts were announced then she might have worried a little, because if ever the devil stared out of a girl's eyes in St Begh's, he did on that day. The play was of course a huge success, as it always would be; Mary-Anne looked spectacular in the blue dress and shawl, but Kathleen had to wear a strange rough costume of sacking, an ass's head of papier mache and make "hee-haw" noises. Here the germs of jealousy and hatred took root, grew and flourished.

Girls are cruel; far more cruel than boys, who show their dislike overtly in blows and shouting. Girls' cruelty is more subtle and insidious. Kathleen Hegarty lived on Windmill Brow, closer to the other members of their group than Mary-Anne. She saw them during the Christmas holidays whilst Mary-Anne, on the other side of town, did not. When Mary-Anne returned to school in January 1887 she skipped over to where her friends were gathered around Kathleen, but to her astonishment they started giggling and whispering behind their hands while looking at her. She knew well enough what this meant for her group had dished out this treatment to people they did not like often enough. Kathleen Hegarty looked directly at her and said that some people got ideas above themselves and stuck their noses in the air. Millicent Tumelty said loudly and to no one in particular that some girls were no better than they should be, a peculiarly hurtful phrase that her mother was fond of using though she was not sure entirely of its meaning. Mary-Anne thus found that her friends had deserted her and that none of the other girls in the class would speak to her for fear of Kathleen, who had a vicious streak that manifested in physical violence of a quite random nature. Mary-Anne, once a bystander to this spite now found herself its object. Her hair would be sharply pulled while standing in line; a foot would be stuck out in class causing her to trip, and more and more she was the recipient of actual blows. These did not just come as slaps, but punches in her back and forceful shoving in the corridors. She did not dare to hit back for the bigger girl was quite capable of doing her great damage as she well knew and she was very afraid of her. Equally sure it was that she could not appeal to Sister Thomas Aquinas or Sister Mary Magdalene, because then she would be a sneak and her life would become so much worse, though it hardly could be. Those who told would be followed around the yard and the streets by a chanting juvenile mob:

'Tell tale tit,
Your tongue will be split
And all the little doggies in the town shall have a bit.'

The worst thing though was the corrosive dislike and whispering of her former friends who now walked on the other side of the yard or road and who whispered and giggled while looking at her. Words would drift across, deliberately loud to ensure that she heard, 'slut,' 'slattern,' 'bitch' and so on. In prayers Father Murphy led the school in hopes of heaven, but Mary-Anne knew that she already lived in hell. It was not long before she stopped going to school on several days a week, feigning illness. Of course, her stepmother knew that there was nothing wrong with her, but was trying to build a relationship with the girl so wrote her notes. The excuses grew thinner and thinner and the nuns grew more sceptical with each absence, but soon Mary-Anne stopped going altogether. By mid May of 1887 she was not going to school at all. She did not wish to roam the streets, however; Whitehaven can be a cold and rainy town and it was more comfortable at home. The truth was that Mary-Anne was well aware of her ascendancy, and the older woman was no more capable of making her go to school than she herself was of fighting Kathleen Hegarty. Mary-Anne did not tell Rose Anne of the bullying she was receiving partly through shame and partly because her nature rebelled against telling her stepmother anything. That she was guilty of treating Rose Anne in a similar fashion to the way she was being treated herself did not occur to her. John Connelly set out for work every morning and as far as he was aware, his daughter was going to school. His young wife did not tell him the truth because she was ashamed of what she saw as her own failing in not managing to get Mary-Anne to go to St Begh's and knew that he would be angry if told; it was easier to say nothing.

As a parent John Connelly was obliged by law to ensure that his daughter attended school. When the first letter arrived from the school committee stating that Mary-Anne was not attending at St Begh's it came as a surprise. When he questioned Rose Anne the truth came out.

'So how long has she been staying at home now?'

'About six weeks John.'

'And you let her?'

Rose Anne had no response to this; Connelly was as blind to her powerlessness in the matter as he was to his daughter's treatment of his wife. It was an inconvenience that he did not want. Like many men of his time and circumstances he did not see it as his role to take his daughter in hand, so foolishly he did not speak to Mary-Anne himself. She was the apple of his eye, but it was Rose Anne's duty to send her to school and keep house. In this, to his mind, she was failing as a wife just as much as she was as housekeeper. The letter reminded him that he had a duty to send his daughter to school and that there would be a penalty to pay if he failed to do this. Accordingly, he instructed Rose Anne to ensure that his daughter went to school and left it at that, secure in the knowledge that his word would be obeyed.

On Saturday 28 May 1887 John Connelly went to work as usual. He spent the morning beating plates into curved shapes for making a ship's boiler. It was hot, hard and heavy work and when he had finished at 12.30pm he went to the Dusty Miller, where he met Sal Madge and her group of friends to talk and play cards. His drinking was moderate and during his one and a half hour stay in the pub he drank only four pints. Growing maudlin and sentimental, he chose the moment to announce that he was going to be a father again.

'When did you find this out John?'

'Just this morning Sal, before work.'

'Are you pleased?'

'Why should I not be?'

'Well from what you've been saying I thought you and her were not getting on that well.'

'Oh, we've had some hard words, but she is my wife after all.'

'Well perhaps you'd better try to be nicer to her in the future.'

'Aye well, maybe you're right.'

'New babby and all that; she'd better cut down on't drink though. That nivver does babbies any good, thou noz.'

'True enough.'

'Get her some flowers.'

'Eh?'

'Get her some flowers. Women like flowers.'

'How would you know that Sal; been giving any women flowers?' interpolated John Kennedy.

'Cheeky bugger; you watch thy step my lad or I'll skelp thee yan,' replied Sal, pretending to lash out at Kennedy as he ducked.

'What flowers do you suggest then Sal?'

'Well I would say daffodils, but it's past time of year for them. Just get what you can afford on the market. That'll put her in a good mood I should think.'

'I didn't know you liked flowers Sal,' said Isaac Tyson.

'There's lots of things you don't know about me marra; but yis I like flowers. Daffodils especially; they're my favourites.'

'Why's that Sal?'

'Wordsworth.'

'What; the poet? Yis he did a poem on daffodils didn't he?'

'He did and I like that. " And then my heart with pleasure fills, and dances with the daffodils". But I liked him too. We get a lot of daffs up along the railway in spring you know.'

'What's that; did you meet him then?'

'Yis I did, but it was years and years ago mind. He used to come to Whitehaven a lot. His son lived up at Moresby. He were the vicar or summat.'

'So how did you meet him?'

'Up at the incline. He came up one day, told me who he was, and was asking how things worked so I told him. He gave me a half crown for telling him. I liked the man so I was more inclined to like his poems. The one about Whitehaven I thought was beautiful.'

'He wrote a poem about Whitehaven? I never knew that.'

'I think a lot of folk don't; but it was more part of Whitehaven. He wrote it about a high spot on the coast between Moresby and Whitehaven so I reckon it was Bransty Hill.'

'Well there's worse things to write poetry about than Bransty.'

'True enough. Can you remember any of it?'

'Aye, just a bit though. I can't think of it all. I did trouble to learn it because it was about here, but I've forgotten half of it.'

'Well let's hear that bit then.'

'Yis; go on Sal, gis a bit of verse.'

Sal Madge screwed her face up in the effort of memory and began:

'*The Sun, that seemed so mildly to retire,*
Flung back from distant climes a streaming fire,
Whose blaze is now subdued to tender gleams,
Prelude of night's approach, with soothing dreams.
Look round - of all the clouds not one is moving;
'Tis the still hour of thinking, feeling, loving.
Silent, and stedfast as the vaulted sky,
The boundless plain of waters seems to lie -
Comes that low sound from breezes rustling o'er
The grass crowned headland that conceals the shore?'

'That's it. That's all I can bring to mind.'

'And that's Bransty?'

'That's right John.'

'It is though, isn't it?' said Isaac. 'It's Bransty at sunset. That's just what it's like. He had a way with words though didn't he? That's summat that is.'

'What did he look like?' asked John Connelly.

'Look like? Well when I saw him first I thought he looked a bit daft.'

'Why was that?'

'Well his clothes were a bit out of date, if you know what I mean. He had on stripy trousers and a brown jacket and had that slight mad about the eyes look you see sometimes. He walked along sort of rolling, a bit like a sailor. But then I saw he had a good face.'

'You can tell if someone's good by their face?'

'No. A good strong nose I meant, and he looked like he laughed a lot. I thought he was a bit posh at first but when I got talking to him there was no doubt about where he came from. Cumbrian accent right enough. He looked like he spent a lot of time outdoors and more than owt else he reminded me of an old shepherd.'

'A shepherd?'

'Aye. I think I liked him because his face looked like an old hoss.'

'No wonder you liked him then! You like hosses.'

'I do that.'

John Connelly left the pub happy, but steady on his feet; on his way he took a detour to the Market Place where he bought a bunch of roses for Rose Anne to make her happy. When he got home he found her drunk, having consumed half a bottle of gin. That would have to change, he thought as he presented her with the flowers and a kiss; time for a new era. She on her part also had reason that day to make John Connelly happy. To make him so and to keep him that way she had taken two large ewers down the lane and had them filled; each of these held half a gallon of strong beer. He did not know that, but reacted with pleasure when she served him with four pints one after the other; she kept him company by drinking gin as if it were going out of fashion. It was just as she went to get his third pint that she gave him the letter.

Chapter 9

A Woman of Valour

John Connelly had now consumed seven pints but being a seasoned drinker it had not fuddled him so that he could not read the letter from the Whitehaven School Board. It informed him once again that his daughter had not been attending school, reminded him that there were penalties accruing to such an offence, and then stated flatly that they had notified the magistrates. Connelly would be summoned to answer why Mary-Anne had not been going to St Begh's and could expect to be fined heavily. In the meantime, they urged him in the strongest possible terms to send his daughter to school and to pay the fine they were imposing upon him of five shillings, the maximum they were allowed to levy without going to court. To Connelly this amount was quite heavy enough and he grew very angry, bellowing at Rose Anne.

'What the hell is this? I told you to make sure Mary-Anne went to school did I not?'

His wife immediately burst into tears, but her voice came weak and slurred from the amount of gin she had consumed.

'I couldn't help it John. I can't make her.'

'What do you mean, you can't make her? She's a laal lass for God's sake. Of course you can make her!'

'I cannot John. She's got a mind of her own and she will not do as I say.'

'Will not do as you say? Then you make her. But you won't will you you lazy bitch? Look at this spot; I work hard and come home and this house is like a bloody hovel.'

'I'm sorry John; I cannot help it.'

'Cannot? Will not you mean you slut. I come home every day to find you've been drinking my money away, no dinner on the table and now this!'

This exchange was delivered in an enraged bellow by a man convinced he was being unjustly used and in the full richness of drunken self-righteousness. It is hardly surprising that it was heard through the thin walls of the cheap terraced housing, and, the day being warm, through the open window onto the street.

'I don't know why I married you. I must have been mad; when I think of the way Maggie used to keep the house. She didn't drink herself sodden, leave the place in filth, and aye, she sent my lad to school with never a bother nor any damned fines!'

This was almost too much for the verbally battered wife.

'You said that you loved me, and I believed you. That's why we got married.'

Connelly's response was a retort, 'The more fool me!'

Stung by his callousness, Rose Anne grew defensive; the drink making her bold.

'I wish I hadn't married you too, John Connelly, for I was a lot happier before I met you. I had a job, prospects, money in my pocket and no nasty little cow making my life miserable while you spend your hours at the pub.'

'Mary-Anne a nasty little cow?' Connelly's voice rose again into a full-throated bellow of rage. 'Don't you speak of my daughter that way or I'll make you sorry for it. You learn your place woman and don't give me any of your backchat. I am master here.'

'Then make your daughter go to school, because she takes no notice of me at all.'

'That's your job. You are the woman of the house. I go out to work for the money. I pay the rent, I put money on the table and you do bugger all. You take notice of what I say; you get that lass to school on Monday or I'll take the back of my hand to you.'

'You wouldn't dare!'

'Oh, wouldn't I?' shouted Connelly. 'If that girl is not in school on Monday then I swear to you by the holy mother of God that I'll lather you to within an inch of your life with this. Just see if I don't.'

Connelly grabbed a thick walking stick from the corner and brought it down onto their rough plank table with a crash, at which Rose Anne screamed.

Listeners in the street and on either side heard the bellow, the crash and the scream and looked at each other.

'Has he murdered her?'

The question was soon answered.

Utterly distraught, Rose Anne ran into the street and made her way off down the road on very unsteady legs. There may have been some sighs of relief among the neighbours that there had not been a murder, but her condition caused no particular comment. Women the worse for drink were a common sight in this part of town.

Rose Anne made her unsteady way to the Market Place where she bought some potatoes, some mince and a cabbage. Tatties, mince and greens were one of Connelly's favourite meals; perhaps she could put him back in a good mood through proving that she could cook him what he liked. The new Market Hall had been built in 1880 and was an impressive looking modern building; behind it, however, were some very old lanes running down to the harbour and in one of these she bought a small bottle of that which ruins mothers. When she returned home, Connelly was still in the front room and still drinking beer, having found the ewers in the scullery. Mary-Anne was nowhere to be seen, she having gone out to see a girl she knew further up the street. John Connelly seemed to have forgotten the row they had just had; indeed he had forgotten most things. He had taken a lot of strong beer on an empty stomach and was now approaching the state where he either stood or sat and stared into space. Never a violent drunk, this zombie like condition would last until he lay down somewhere and went to sleep. Seeing that her husband was in no mood for food Rose Anne decided to have some more gin. By six o'clock in the evening she was running out of this vital commodity and regretting that she had not bought a larger bottle in the first place, so she slipped out to a small shop a few doors down from her house and bought some more. It was not any spirit that duty had been paid on.

At just after seven o'clock that evening Elizabeth Atkinson of number 2 Albion Street, just down the road from Rosemary Lane, was making dinner for her husband, a plumber, who was out on a job and due back. Her daughter Lucy came running in off the street to tell her that Mr Connelly's house was on fire. There were also shouts in the street of 'Fire! Fire!' Mrs Atkinson moved her pans to the side of the range and immediately ran over the road to where thick black smoke was pouring out of the open front door of Connelly's house. From the step she could see Rose Anne lying on the fire; her skirt was burned completely off and the upper part of her clothes were all in flames. Mrs Atkinson screamed, but the smoke was so thick that neither she nor any of the onlookers dared to enter the room, for who would be foolhardy enough to rush into a burning house? There was no sign of John Connelly anywhere. Later, Mrs Atkinson was to attest that two young men arrived and did what was necessary; her eyes were weeping from thick oily smoke and she could not see properly. In actual fact, it was Sal Madge and John Kennedy who had finished their drinks and cards and were walking up Rosemary Lane when they saw what was happening as smoke billowed in thick black clouds out of the windows and doors of a house.

'That's John Connelly's spot on fire.'

'Aye; we'd better have a look.'

A small knot of people were outside the Connelly house talking excitedly but none had the courage to go through into the front room to attempt a rescue of anyone in there. Sal Madge looked into the door and through thick smoke she dimly saw Rose Anne lying across the fire which was burning brightly. Extraordinary times call for extraordinary people; Sal did not hesitate, but took her kerchief from round her neck and wrapped up to cover her nose and mouth; John Kennedy did likewise.

Horrified at the risk she was about to take one of the neighbourhood men placed himself in front of her.

'Nay Sal; don't ga in thear. You'll be roasted to death.'

'Do you pay my wages Jimmy Moynes?'

Puzzled he replied, 'Nay I don't'.

'Then you don't get to tell me what to do, do you? Now you can either step aside or I'll knock you out o't way. Tek thee pick.'

Abashed, he fell back and she walked calmly into the smoke vomiting out of the door, followed by John Kennedy. Crossing the room, holding her breath, Sal blenched at what she saw; Connelly's wife was literally frying in front of her and flat out unconscious. The smoke in the room was thick and there was a stench of burning flesh. Kennedy retched, but Sal looked at him sternly and motioned to grab Rose Anne's arm. She was lying part on the fender and part in the fire; with one heave they rolled her off these and onto the floorboards which were wet. Forced to catch some sort of breath Sal briefly gagged as the thick greasy smoke took her in the throat, and strained not to breathe as her eyes watered and it became difficult to see. Then Kennedy took Rose Anne's burned feet and Sal her shoulders and they carried her out into the street where they laid her down as they gasped for the good air.

The women waiting in the street screamed at the sight, crossing themselves and someone said; 'Holy Mary, mother of God!' Men stood and stared aghast. Sal Madge rose to her feet and went to go back into the house. That entering a house she thought to be ablaze was an act of the rashest form of courage did not seem to occur to her. She entirely missed the expressions in the eyes of the onlookers which spoke of awe at what they had just witnessed.

'Mary-Anne's not at home, Sal. She's not here,' said one of the women.

'That's summat then,' replied Sal grimly. 'I don't have to go upstairs in that stife. Now send a lad to get a doctor as fast as he can.'

'Is she still alive?'

'Aye she is; God knows how, but she is.'

Within a minute a local boy was pelting down the road to fetch the nearest medical practitioner, Dr Irwin.

Just then Connelly appeared in the doorway of the house, his eyes staring, his walk unsteady. He had been out in the back yard and had just walked through the smoky house. His hands looked burned and his trouser legs were wet, the upper parts smouldering and giving off smoke.

'What has happened here, Mr Connelly?' One of the neighbours made the enquiry.

'I wouldn't expect any answers,' said Sal Madge. 'He's had a skinful and won't make any sense until he's slept it off.'

'What shall we do with him?'

'Prop him up by the door and get someone to put out that fire. We've got to get this lass to Howgill Street.'

By now it had become apparent that it was not the house that had been on fire, but the unfortunate woman now lying on the street outside.

Just then three men came running up the hill led by Edward Parker. They were very much the worse for drink and wanted to see what was going on. Sal Madge could see that they were drunk and that they were yelling excitedly, but she had more on her mind than dealing with drunks, so took no notice of them. Parker attempted to go into the house and this roused Connelly whose instinct to defend his home was present even in his almost automaton state.

'Where d'you think you're going?' Connelly put his arm out to stop Parker.

'In to have a look,' replied Parker and tried to shove his way past. Connelly's aggression was roused and he pushed Parker back with a hand on his chest. However, Parker had two other men with him and they shoved their way in and Connelly sat down by the door on the cobbles. One of the drunks went upstairs. Parker's attention was distracted by the arrival of a man from the Manx Arms who had brought a stretcher normally used sometimes by customers to get their friends home when they were incapable. It may have gone through Parker's head that he could appear to be the hero of the hour, but whatever his motive, he grabbed the stretcher and brought it over to where the burned woman was lying. Sal Madge knew nothing of this as her attention was on nothing except Rose Anne; when the stretcher arrived she neither knew nor cared who had brought it, but assisted to lay Mrs Connelly on it. Dr Irwin came running up the hill, bag in hand and was soon kneeling down by the stretcher looking at the stricken woman. He drew his breath in sharply.

'Good God! We must get her to the infirmary as soon as possible.'

Sal Madge nodded her approval; she and Kennedy with John Kendall, one of the drunks, and a man from the neighbouring houses each took a handle of the stretcher and then they carried Rose Anne, mercifully covered with a blanket provided by a kindly woman, directly to the infirmary in Howgill Street. Dr Irwin went into the house that was, by now, mostly clear of smoke. He saw nothing to engage his professional attention and went upstairs to check that there was no one injured up there.

Whitehaven's infirmary was a charitable foundation which had been open since 1830. It was very generously endowed in the wills of several wealthy local people, and especially by baroness de Sternberg, who left enough money to set up what she called a 'Samaritan Fund'. Through this, the poor could be taken in at the infirmary, receive treatment and pay nothing. Thus Rose Anne was received at the door by starched nurses and porters and was soon laid out on a bed under the gaze of Dr Muriel, a prominent local GP, who gave of his time freely to help poorer people in need of medical assistance. Sal Madge and John Kennedy then made their ways back home.

Rose Anne was still unconscious, which was just as well; her clothing was burned onto her, but within a few minutes and under the direction of the doctor, she was laid into a warm bath and allowed to soak for a few minutes. This was the standard treatment for what the profession termed 'a crinoline accident'; these were very common occurrences. Once the stiffened burn and blood on her had softened the nurses peeled off her clothing and such burnt material as they could. Then they dried her by patting with flannel and then applied cotton wadding to the burned areas that covered most of her body; this was kept in place with bandages; the dressings would be changed after four days, when it would need to be soaked off. The gin had at least been kind to her for she knew nothing of this and stayed dead to the world throughout the whole process apart from a few moans. Dr Muriel and the nurses had smelled her breath and knew the cause of her state very well.

It is necessary now to retrace our steps to the moment that Sal Madge and her companions had left the Connelly household with their patient for the infirmary. Two drunken men had forced their way past Connelly into the house; it was now that the police arrived. Edward Parker had not yet entered the house, but as he saw the two policemen hurrying up Rosemary Lane he stepped inside the door, so that when they arrived it was he that they saw first. The onlookers in the street disappeared; many of them had no liking for the police. One of Parker's two associates, Kendall, had gone to the infirmary, but now Richard Walker came down beside him and to him he said, 'Back me up. It's time for someone to get his come-uppance.'

As PC Mouatt pounded up to the scene, Parker stepped out, pointing at Connelly and said to the constable, 'That's him. He put his wife on the fire and tried to kill her.'

Sergeant Hope who had arrived just after Mouatt said, 'What's that? He put his wife on the fire? What do you mean? First of all, put some bloody water on his trousers; he's smoking down there.'

This was done quickly with a bucket of water held by one of the bystanders.

'Right; what do you mean?' repeated Hope.

'I saw him. There was smoke coming out of the house so I went through the door and I saw him holding his wife onto the fire. He was trying to burn her to death.'

'Good God!' cried Hope, looking at Connelly, whose trousers were now soaked. 'Is this true?'

Connelly said nothing, but leaned against the wall, staring into space, sunk again into catatonic drunkenness.

'Aye it's true,' said Parker. 'I saw him doing it and there's another witness too.' Here he nudged Walker. 'You saw it too didn't you marra?'

Walker said nothing, but nodded in affirmation that what Parker said was true.

'Was it you that stopped him?' asked PC Mouatt.

'No it was some young chap ran in and grabbed him by the throat throttling him. Then he gave over and came out here. Now we want to give him in charge. Are you going to arrest him?'

'Just watch me! What's his name?'

'He's called John Connelly; he's a blacksmith at Ramsay's down the road.'

Hope signalled to PC Mouatt who produced a pair of handcuffs.

'I don't care if he's the grand panjandrum of Workington; he's under arrest. What's his wife called?'

'Her name's Rose Anne, so I understand.'

'Is she badly burned?'

'Very much so, Sergeant,' said Dr Irwin, coming out of the house from where he had been listening by the door. 'If that is what he did then he practically turned her to charcoal.'

'But she's still alive?'

'As far as I know.'

The sergeant turned to Connelly, 'John Connelly, I am arresting you on a suspicion that you have committed grievous bodily harm upon the person of your wife, Rose Anne Connelly. You must accompany me to the police station. Cuff him Mouatt. Now gentlemen, this will go to court; you will be called to give evidence, so I shall need a few particulars from you.'

Parker could scarcely contain his glee as he and his companions gave their names and addresses.

Connelly made no resistance as he was handcuffed and led away down the hill between the two policemen. Within twenty minutes he was booked in at the desk and Hope was relating to Superintendent Thornburrow the story that he had been told. The superintendent listened to what he had to say, then asked the leading question.

'Do we know the condition of the unfortunate woman?'

'Not yet sir; there has not been time to enquire.'

'Then, Sergeant, I suggest that you make your way to the infirmary and ascertain what it is. You have arrested this man on suspicion of causing grievous bodily harm, but I cannot charge him without knowing exactly what the harm is. You must go and see her Sergeant and ask the doctors what the extent of her injuries may be. Take Mouatt with you.'

Sergeant Hope was soon standing before Dr Muriel; his tone was most deferential in asking what the condition of Mrs Connelly might be; the doctor was a very well respected person in the district.

'I fear Sergeant that she is in a very grave state. I have attended many cases of burns in my career, but never one as severe as this. She is burned over seventy per cent of her body, and her feet are so charred as to be almost burned off. It is a miracle that she is still alive; I would not have thought that such a case could still sustain life.'

'Is she going to live sir?'

The doctor looked thoughtful, 'I could never say for certain that such a patient will die; she might live. But I have to say that I think she will die and very soon. She is unconscious still, and from the smell of her breath that is down to alcohol. Sooner or later she will wake and when she does then the likelihood is that either shock or tetanus will kill her very quickly.'

'Will she be in pain if she wakes, sir?'

'Some, I have no doubt, but burns are sometimes merciful in destroying nerves. Certainly if she moves there will be great pain; but if she lies still then perhaps not as much as might be thought.'

'It would be merciful then sir if she did not awake.'

'I do not disagree with that Sergeant. Even if this poor woman recovers, she would be so scarred and disfigured that as far as the human race is concerned she would be a monster, a freak to hide in the shadows and for the ignorant to taunt.'

'May I see her, sir?'

'What for?'

'I have to make a report to my superintendent sir.'

'Very well; but make it quick; come with me.'

Shown up to where Rose Anne lay wrapped in cotton wadding and bandages, Hope whistled at the sight and made a few notes.

As Dr Muriel led them down the steps out onto Howgill Street Sergeant Hope spoke to him one more time.

'I must be quite clear when making my report Doctor; my apologies for repeating the question, but I must ask again; you think she is unlikely to live?'

'And I repeat Sergeant that my professional opinion is that she is likely to die and within a very short time.'

'Thank you, sir'

Sergeant Hope hurried back to Whitehaven police station to relate his news to Thornburrow.

'You can charge him sir; grievous bodily harm; no doubts of it.'

'And two witnesses to it. Seems like an open and shut case to me Sergeant, but you do realise what it may become don't you?'

'Sir?'

'If this unfortunate woman dies then, although we have him in the cells for grievous bodily harm, it will be murder.'

Hope looked at his superior for a moment as the statement sunk in.

'We haven't had a murder for a very long time, sir.'

'No, indeed. And to bring it to trial in such a short time would look very well for us, Sergeant.'

'It would sir; but I hope the lady lives.'

'So do I, Sergeant; but if she does not then we already have the culprit bang to rights. Good work.'

Thornburrow's eyes gleamed a little; this could be what he had been waiting for; his professional cherry on the cake. Carefully he set out the details of the case and placed it into the file of matters to be brought before the magistrates on Monday. It would have to be circulated around the local solicitors of course; the man Connelly would need to be defended, but this was open and shut. It would need to be handled carefully and matters would have to wait on events, but should the situation change then the gentlemen of the local press must be informed. Down in the cells John Connelly slumbered heavily, sleeping off his excesses; in the infirmary Rose Anne hovered in a twilight between life and death. One of them would certainly wake in the morning; his fate appeared to depend on whether the other did too.

Chapter 10

Mr Atter is Sceptical

Sal Madge knew nothing of Connelly's arrest. After delivering Rose Anne to the infirmary, she and John Kennedy had made their way back to Rosemary Lane, but, it being Saturday evening, many of the locals were indulging their favourite weekend pursuit and the pubs were full; there were no spectators outside the house which had been locked up. There was no sign of life within and Sal assumed that Connelly and his daughter had gone to the infirmary; thus she and Kennedy went up the hill heading for Windmill and passed the rest of the evening convivially in an ale house.

Next morning, it was the Sabbath and a day of rest; Sal did not go to work. It was a fine June day with a blue sky and the weather promised to be warm. This being so, she decided to indulge in one of her favourite pastimes, which had the extra advantage of adding to her purse. Living with her and sharing her bed was a character who has been mentioned previously in this story, who went by the name of Flirt. This was a small red-brown spaniel cross mongrel of indeterminate breeding who was the apple of Sal Madge's eye. When asked why she had called her dog Flirt, she would always answer with a gleam in her eye.

'Because he is.'

'A flirt, Sal? Your dog's a flirt?'

'Oh aye - he'll flirt with owt he will. He's a devil with the lasses is he.'

If anyone had suggested to Sal the possibility that she might be projecting something of her own desires or feelings onto her dog, they would have got short shrift. However, the dog was, according to her, very special; there was no dog like him. The reason for this hyperbole was the terrier's love of, and talent in the art of diving. There was a slipway down into the water near one of the quays and when the tide was in there was a good depth right by it. Flirt loved to swim, being, like most dogs, very fond of a good splash. Sal had discovered, when the dog was little more than a pup, that if she threw something into the water then he would retrieve it in double quick time. Best of all was that if something sank and the water was clear, the dog would dive to the bottom and bring the object up and onto land. Sal had cobbled together a number of sticks with weights attached to them to make them sink. She would set her hat by the edge of the water and if anyone wished to see Flirt dive, they would put a farthing in the hat and in return would receive a stick to throw. On Sundays, when the port was not working as much as during the week, many of the well to do would stroll round the quays to see what might be seen and their children found Sal's improvised diversion very amusing. She was such a well known local character that their parents were happy to oblige with as many farthings as Flirt would with dives. Ultimately, Sal would judge the matter and call a halt when she decided that Flirt had done enough.

'That's it now; I don't want to tire him out; that would never do now would it?'

She would often assert with glee that 'there's no dog like him; no dog like him!' This was undoubtedly true for all dogs are unique in themselves, but it gave her considerable satisfaction to repeat it to all who would listen. If there were few things in her life that were special, then Flirt certainly was one of them.

It was not unusual of her to think of the welfare of animals, because it was in her nature. With human beings who crossed her she could be as hard as nails and unbending; in some cases the retribution she visited on people was swift and decisive. With animals it was the reverse and everyone knew it. It did not matter what the beast was, be it dog, cat, horse, duck, goose or whatever variety, she had a gentleness towards them and a belief that they responded far more to kindness than to cruelty. This applied to children too, and in this she was unusual. She lived in a community that used force against its children on a daily basis to enforce its will. Her own childhood had been subject to the occasional clout or clip round the ear, but she knew of children near her who were beaten every single day and she did not approve. She could not interfere of course; humans were things of reason and if a parent beat their own child she knew that she could not intervene, however much she wanted to for she had no right. With animals it was a very different thing.

Once she was walking down George Street in the more fashionable end of town and she came across a wagoner thrashing his horse. She stopped and looked at the wagon with a professional eye; it was loaded with sacks of grain; then she spoke to the man.

'Thou'll give owwer skelping that beast I hope.'

'Why the devil should I?' The man snarled, for he was a stranger and did not know who was speaking to him.

You've got one hoss and a wagon with twelve bushels of wheat is why.'

'What of it?'

'You know as well as I do, marra. That hoss is overloaded and he's had enough.'

'I'm not your marra, you maff bitch. Mind your own bloody business.'

'Standard load is six bushels you lazy bugger and yon hoss is carrying for two, most likely to save you going back and forth to the mill.'

'I've telt you to mind your own business man-woman, so sod off and mind it or thou'll get what this bastard's getting.'

There was a disapproving murmur from the onlookers, but the wagoner did not care; the power to do as he wished was firmly in his mind; Sal just spat some tobacco juice onto the ground. He turned back to thrash the horse again; he did not succeed. The whip was grabbed by Sal who wrenched it from his hand. Surprised he snarled again, 'Right you've bloody asked for it.'

The answer took him by surprise; Sal had been using a whip for decades and was an artist at making the lash go exactly where she wished. It caught him on the face and he was unsighted, raising his hands to defend his eyes, as she knew he would. Then she commenced to thrash him with the whip to delighted exclamations from the people around. Desperately, he tried to close with her and to disarm her; when she was quite ready, she let him, and as he drew within reach knocked him to the floor where he lay groaning.

'You were taking this to the mill?'

'Aye.'

He was soundly beaten and knew it. Sal looked up and flagged down a passing empty wagon driven by a man she knew. With the help of bystanders six bushels of wheat were transferred to the empty wagon, then both went to the mill to deliver their loads.

'If I ever see you treating a hoss like that agyan, I'll throw thee into t'dock. Understand?'

He understood; he had met Sal Madge.

Let us return to the Sunday morning after the Connelly house fire as Flirt had finished the last of his dives; it was approaching midday and Sal was seeking out a friend of hers. Like many Whitehovians, Sal was very fond of a wild goose that lived in the harbour. This creature was white, large and although friendly to humans, was very noisy. The locals had decided that it made such a row that the only possible name for it was Barney because it certainly raised one of those if it was offered any titbits. This was many years before a gentleman living in the town decided to replace the now dead wild goose with a tame one which he also named Barney. Sal was offering the goose a crust of bread and he was advancing towards her with raucous calls of approval, when out of the corner of her eye she saw the well-known figure of Mr Edward Atter walking in her direction.

Mr Atter was somewhat perturbed in his mind this morning; for one thing he had not been to church, and had decided that he would attend the evening service instead. The reason for his departure from his usual routine had been the arrival of a buff envelope by the hand of a constable dispatched to him by Superintendent Thornburrow which contained the cases which were to be brought up before the magistrates on the following morning. The usual litany of Saturday night drunks and minor assaults held little interest for him, but the charge brought against Connelly was an entirely different order of things. Atter knew Whitehaven well and had a very good idea where he could find Sal Madge with whom he wished to have a few minutes of conversation. Now he approached her where she squatted down to feed Barney the goose. He stood near her; Sal knew who he was, but did not think that he had come to speak to her, so simply stood up, to see him watching her.

'Miss Madge, I must ask your indulgence, for we have not been introduced, but I would be very glad of a few minutes of your time.'

'Well Mr Atter, air is free and I am at my leisure so please speak thy piece.'

Atter was pleased at his reception and his mind registered with approval that there was no hint of subservience in her tone; she had spoken to him as an equal, so he proceeded in that frame.

'I understand that you attended at a fire yesterday evening, though I am not clear what your part in the matter was.'

'I did.'

'Very well. I have to say that we must not actually discuss what occurred because the matter is *sub judice*, but I would be very glad to hear from you an account of what happened at the house of Mr and Mrs Connelly yesterday.'

'Sub youdickey; what's that? Thou must pardon my ignorance Mr Atter, but I am not in thy line of work.'

Atter thought that it would be a grave mistake to take this as an admission of ignorance; he had the impression that he was dealing with someone of great wisdom, who carried herself with the same air as had many of the rich and aristocratic clients he had dealings with.

'I do apologise; it means that the matter is subject to legal proceedings in which you may be involved. That being the case, I must not actually talk to you about it, but would be glad to hear the bare account of what happened last night. I would be grateful if you could relate the events to me, what you saw and who was present.'

Sal nodded, 'Is someone in trouble?'

'Yes; Mr Connelly has been arrested.'

Atter made a noncommittal gesture, 'I may take the case.'

'But you want to hear from me so you can decide?'

Atter signalled his agreement with a slight smile.

'Aye alright; sit yourself down on that bollard and I'll have this one.'

It did not take Sal Madge long to relate what had happened and to describe her part in matters. When she had done, Atter nodded. 'Thank you. That makes the thing much clearer in my mind.'

'You'll take his case up?'

'I rather think I will, though I will see him as well before I decide.'

'You think John Connelly will go to prison?'

'I fear that it could be much worse than that if the poor woman dies. There are some who say that he burned her deliberately.'

Sal's eyes opened wider, 'They'll say he murdered her?'

'I think it likely; you must be prepared to give evidence, but for the moment I would be glad if you would keep your thoughts to yourself and our conversation private.'

'You have my word on it.'

Edward Atter looked at Sal Madge and knew that he could go to the bank with such a promise from her. Touching the brim of his hat to her with his thanks, he departed, leaving her deep in speculation and wonder. Walking swiftly, he turned his steps towards Whitehaven police station where waited a man who he knew might be facing the hangman's noose before too long. Atter had reservations about taking the case on until he had heard Connelly's story from his own lips, because he thought he might be out of his depth. If things were the way Thornburrow had outlined in his message to local solicitors then Connelly would be in need of a far bigger legal gun than he could provide. When he was shown downstairs and into the cell where Connelly sat, thickheaded and hung over on a plank bed folded down from the wall, Atter sat down beside him.

Connelly's mood was very low, because he had never been in a cell before. He was Irish and Catholic and his view of his own situation was far from positive. He had reason to be gloomy, for the Fenian Brotherhood who sought to free Ireland from the British government and set up a republic had been carrying out a campaign of dynamite bombings through the 1880s which had skewed the view of the English population against the Irish community. Irish and Catholic had both been demonised in the newspapers whilst the Orange movement was extremely strong in Whitehaven. He had already been called a 'paddy bastard' by one constable and had little faith that an English court was going to be sympathetic to him. Part of his mind convinced him that he had already been found guilty of harming his wife. Edward Atter spoke to him gently.

'You appear to be in a great deal of trouble, Connelly.'

'So they've told me sir, but I hope that you can get me out of it. I didn't do what they say I did.'

'What exactly have they accused you of?'

'They say I done grievous bodily harm to Rose Anne, Mr Atter; but I'd never do that.'

'I understand that you were somewhat the worse for drink when you were arrested. Can you remember what happened yesterday?'

'Only bits of it. I'm sorry sir, but I did have a bit of a skinful.'

'Very well. Please tell me what parts you can remember about how your wife came to be burned.'

'Well, like I said it's a bit muzzy, but I was sitting at the table and it was a bit dark in the room. The lamp was on the mantelpiece you see and the glass got sooted.'

'Ah; so the room was very dim; was it the only source of light?'

'No sir. The fire was lit, but a bit low, and Rose Anne went to attend to the lamp. I think she found the oil was low.'

'Paraffin oil?'

'Yes, sir. I'm not clear how it happened, but next thing I knew was that Rose Anne blazed up; her skirt caught fire and then the rest of her. She went up like a candle.'

'What did you do when this happened?'

'I tried to put it out sir.'

'How did you do that?'

'With my hands; I was beating at it with my hands.'

Here Connelly began to weep.

'Show me your hands please; ah yes, they are rather badly burned. Have they been seen by a doctor?'

'No, sir.'

'What happened then?'

'I was not having much success with the fire so I went into the scullery and there was a bowl of water. I brought that in and threw it over Rose Anne. That put the flames out. The room was dark and the smoke so thick I could not breathe so I went out back.'

'Did you see what happened to your wife?'

'No sir. I think she fell, but I cannot be sure.'

Mr Atter made a few notes in his book.

'It is not for me to judge you, Mr Connelly. You were drunk and because you were drunk your wife has suffered a terrible accident. I believe you, you see; but there are people who say that you held her on the fire and that is why you face the charge of grievous bodily harm. Had you not been drunk and incapable you might have saved her, but that is between you, your conscience and God.'

'It's not true that I held her on the fire Mr Atter. I would never do such a thing.'

'Yes; the problem is that there are two or three witnesses who say that you did. Whatever you may have to say in the matter this makes your case a very serious one.'

'Will I go to prison sir?'

'Not if I have anything to do with it. I shall represent you in court Mr Connelly. I am getting a picture of what happened yesterday which is slightly out of focus, but I fancy that it will become clearer before too long. Now I must go about my business. Do not say anything further to the police about these matters, for they might use your remarks against you. I shall see you tomorrow in court.'

Edward Atter left the police station deep in thought, first instructing that a doctor be called to tend to his client, and stood for a few minutes outside on the pavement, turning over in his mind what he had just heard. Shortly his expression cleared and he set off with a purposeful stride towards Howgill Street. On his arrival at the infirmary he asked if it would be possible to see Mrs Rose Anne Connelly. To his surprise he was told it would not be possible and was asked to wait a few minutes. It was not long before a tall and spare gentleman in clerical dress came up and shook his hand. Atter knew him well for it was the Reverend Richard Duncan who often preached at St Nicholas's church, and who was Chaplain to the infirmary.

'Good afternoon, Edward. I assume that you wish to see Mrs Connelly in connection with the arrest of her husband?'

'Yes, Richard. I am convinced in my own mind that all is not as it appears in this matter and I have decided to take his case on.'

'I understand, but I fear it will not be possible to see Mrs Connelly. She is in a very bad way.'

'Is she conscious?'

'Yes she is, but she is very weak indeed.'

'I need not stress that it is vital that I see her to obtain her version of what happened yesterday. It may well determine whether or not her husband goes to gaol. I know that she is terribly burned, but even a few minutes and even fewer questions may not strain her too much.'

'Oh, but it would Edward. You see it is not just the burns. I'm afraid the poor woman went into premature labour this morning and delivered a stillborn boy child. She has been through a terrible ordeal and is now asleep, which is a mercy.'

Mr Atter looked askance, 'What an awful thing! Is she likely to live?'

The chaplain's manner was grave. 'The doctors think not. She is holding her own at the moment, but if sepsis or tetanus set in the end will come very quickly.'

Edward Atter's thoughts raced into necessary legal channels and came out with the only logical step that he could take to protect his client.

'Is she likely to be awake later today?'

'It is possible, though it would still be best that she not be disturbed in any way.'

Mr Atter looked at him intently, 'Quite to the contrary Richard. At the moment my client is facing a charge of grievous bodily harm. I need not tell you what would follow if Mrs Connelly dies.'

The chaplain's eyes widened. 'Oh. Of course.'

'A man's life will be at stake and we must do what we can to guard it. Whatever else may happen with this unfortunate woman, it is imperative that she must make a sworn statement, so that we may learn from her own lips what happened yesterday evening.'

'You are right, of course; I shall speak to the doctors and make arrangements for you to see her as soon as possible, but I doubt very much that it will be today.'

'No,' said Atter. 'I am the defending solicitor and what you have told me changes the whole thing. The statement must be made to a proper authority and sworn in correct form. I would be obliged if you would arrange with the doctors for Mrs Connelly to be seen tomorrow if at all possible by some legal officers. I shall make the necessary legal arrangements. Let us hope that she lives long enough at least to make a declaration.'

Superintendent Thornburrow had informed the magistrates that a serious case was to come before them, but that he needed a few days to amass his evidence. So John Connelly did not come to court on the Monday following the fire, but was rescheduled to appear on Thursday of that week. For the moment, he languished in the police cells. Edward Atter was not idle, however, and so it was that on the evening of

Monday 30 May Mr John Dickinson, justice of the peace in the county of Cumberland, attended at Whitehaven infirmary. Mr Dickinson was a prominent local businessman whose fulltime occupation was that of auctioneer, a profession at which he prospered, owning the only auction mart in Whitehaven. He was accompanied by Alfred Hooper, the principal clerk to Mr Brockbank, who was, in turn the clerk to the Whitehaven magistrates' court. Also attending was John Connelly, handcuffed and chained to two policemen; he had been told that he must remain silent, though would be allowed to question his wife in due course. They found Mrs Connelly to be awake and in her right mind though very weak; she was able to make a sworn deposition. John Connelly wept at the sight of her and his distress was obvious, as he was allowed to kneel by the bed. When she was able to proceed, Mrs Connelly made her statement in a faint and faltering voice.

'The accused, John Connelly is my husband. About two o'clock on Saturday afternoon last, the 28th May instant, my husband and myself had some unpleasant words about my husband having been fined five shillings for not sending his child to school. He said he thought it hard for him to be fined. I said I could not help it. Shortly afterwards I went into the market, and returned about three o'clock. My husband was in the yard at that time.

Between three and four o'clock I went to the market again and returned in about ten to fifteen minutes. My husband was then sitting reading a newspaper in the house. Between six and seven o'clock I went upstairs for a paraffin lamp. I brought the lamp downstairs and put it on the chimney piece. Some of the oil splashed out down about my arms and on the front of my dress. There was a fire burning in the grate at that time and somehow my dress caught fire. I think my husband was standing at the table at the time. He said "My goodness, what have you done?" I think my husband tried to put out the fire, but I cannot remember. A crowd rushed in. I was in a blaze at the time. I was standing in the room when the crowd came in, but I cannot say in what part of the room. I was burned about the legs, arms and back. My husband had nothing to do with my being burned. My husband and me were on good terms generally, but we fell out sometimes. I don't think my husband was the worse for drink that afternoon, but I think he might have had a pint of ale for dinner.'

When Mrs Connelly had finished speaking her husband was allowed to question her and asked with a pleading tone if she did not remember him trying to put the fire out.

'I think, but I am not sure, you put your arms up and tried to put out the fire. I remember when I had taken fire I ran to the stairs and when I got up two or three steps you said, "My goodness, what has done this?" I mind you pulling my clothes and then the crowd came in. That's all I remember.'

This was all taken down on a triple statement form with two sheets of black carbon paper and the injured woman signed it shakily, her signature being witnessed by Mr Dickinson and Mr Hooper. The original statement was retained for the court; one copy was for Superintendent Thornburrow for the prosecution and the other for the defending solicitor. It was Alfred Hooper who undertook to see that Edward Atter received his copy; he was a clerk in the same solicitor's office as Mr Atter. As a junior, he knew very well that Mr Atter would wish to see the statement as soon as possible, so he made his way over to Bransty with it sealed in an envelope and was shown into Atter's private sitting room. He waited as Edward Atter opened the envelope.

'I think you'll find that it exonerates Mr Connelly, sir; he should walk free immediately.'

Atter made no reply, but read the deposition of Mrs Connelly quickly and as he came to the end he groaned and threw up his hands whilst rolling his eyes.

'I thought you'd like it, sir.'

Atter drew his breath and replied deliberately.

'I do not blame you young man, but this document is of little use to the defence of this poor wretch Connelly. It is hopelessly compromised. What on earth possessed Mr Dickinson to allow the accused man to be in the room while the statement was made?'

'Superintendent Thornburrow thought it best that he be there sir; in his own interests, and of course he could see his wife. He had not seen her since the fire, sir.'

'Oh, indeed. Well listen and learn Mr Hooper. It is very often the case that a woman who has been abused by her husband will blame herself and make excuses for his violence. Have you not come across this before?'

'I have seen it, sir.'

'Quite. Now here we have a woman who probably does not realise that she may die; she will not wish to admit it to herself. Is she likely to incriminate him if she wishes to return to the family home after her discharge from the infirmary? No she is not. But far worse is the presence of her husband; he was looking at her whilst she was making the statement. If she is the sort of woman who blames herself quite needlessly for being abused, how likely is it that she will exonerate her husband if he is looking at her, staring at her? What unseen messages are in their eyes? And that, Mr Hooper, is merely the first flaw.'

'What else is there, sir?'

'The police have three witnesses, now that this wretched man Kendall has come forward, who say something quite different; they say that they saw the woman burning in the fire and that she was being held in it by her husband. Which version is correct? The wife's who was making her deposition, against all legal common sense, in the presence of her husband, or three adult male witnesses? Remember; if this goes to the assizes the jury will be comprised of twelve men. Not a single woman will be sitting in the jury box. And that is not all.'

'Not all, sir?'

'Not by a country mile!' exclaimed Atter. 'There is the testimony of Sal Madge and her version is completely different to the other two. Then there are items in the statement that are risible. Mrs Connelly is trying to give the impression of domestic harmony and respectability. If you read that would you believe that they lived in one of the roughest parts of town? Would you believe that she was drunk? Or that Mr Connelly had consumed I don't know how many pints of strong ale that day? The whole thing is as full of holes as a piece of Nottingham lace. No, I'm afraid, Mr Hooper, that it will not do. Any competent prosecutor would tear that statement into shreds. On present showing John Connelly will be going to prison for a very long time. I must bend my efforts towards ensuring that he does not get sent to the assizes.'

Chapter 11

Truth is Urged

In the days following the horrific burning of Rose Anne Connelly nothing much could happen until Superintendent Thornburrow had completed his investigations. Connelly was to be seen in the magistrates' court on Thursday 2 June, but in the eyes of most of the policemen in the Whitehaven station, he was already guilty. Sergeant Hope and PC Mouatt had heard the statements of Edward Parker, John Kendall and Richard Walker. To them John Connelly was a dyed in the wool villain who had committed a crime so heinous that he deserved nothing but contempt, so that was what he got. To treat a woman in the way that they believed he had done was so unthinkable, so beneath manly virtues that most men in the police station looked forward to him getting his just desserts. Only one policeman in the Whitehaven force had any reservations about the matter and that was PC Thomas Beattie. He was extremely reluctant to believe ill of a man who had helped him out earlier in the year. Beattie might have been more perturbed if he had known at this stage who the chief accuser was, but he was not involved in the case against Connelly and all he knew was that three witnesses had now sworn that the blacksmith had held his wife onto the fire.

The court appearance on Thursday went much as might have been expected. The bench comprised Rev H Fox as chairman, CE Fisher Esq and Rev Canon Dalton. Mr Atter objected to John Connelly being held in a police cell for so long on hearsay evidence, but he was merely going through the form of the thing; he knew that Connelly would not be released at this stage. Superintendent Thornburrow was quite certain that the prisoner had committed an awful crime and he needed time to gather the evidence to press his case. By now this was a matter that could not be dealt with discreetly; someone had leaked the news of the burning wife to the press and newspapers across the country had already judged the thing for themselves. In particular Connelly had been described as behaving with 'atrocious cruelty' and up and down the United Kingdom people were reacting with horror at the actions of a brute beast who could act so within the sacred bonds between husband and wife. If public opinion had been allowed to be the arbiter then Connelly would have been lynched on a wave of public indignation and all would have sworn that he deserved it. In Birmingham, South Shields, Aberdeen and Tonbridge Wells he already stood condemned. Bail was not granted and Thornburrow was given the time he wanted, as he was quite sure that he would have the case for the prosecution prepared by Monday 6 June. Connelly stayed in his cell. The passage of time did make one large difference to his prospects though. On the day after Connelly had been remanded, PC Thomas Beattie sat down in the canteen of the police station with PC Mouatt over a mug of tea and a bun; their conversation turned to the sensational case that was occupying the thoughts of many people in Whitehaven, and indeed the nation.

Edward Atter was well aware that Sal Madge had a considerable status in the town and not just because of her reputation for industry and courage. Strange to tell she had influence up at the castle. It was true that Lord Lonsdale did not reside there much now, preferring the more rural beauty and solitude of Lowther castle not far from Penrith, but his wealth and his power still determined a lot of what went on in the town. Hugh Lowther, the fifth Earl Lonsdale, had come into the earldom in 1882 after the death of his brother from alcoholism. It was in his interests to keep his hand on the pulse of what was going on in the town from which he derived his wealth; he knew very well the story of what had happened back in 1844 when William Lowther, the second earl had inherited the title.

The wealth that William inherited was stupendous along with 75,000 acres of land and a number of palatial residences. Until he inherited the title and estates he had not been well off and, on acceding to the earldom, he had been in a maze of disbelief. One day, shortly after becoming earl, he visited Whitehaven to see what he had got and gazed round at the mines, the fields, the castle and the buildings on his land. Driving along the road was someone he took to be a young man sitting astride a horse and pulling a wagon. In his glee at his new affluence he hailed the wagoner.

'Young man, can you tell me who owns all the land hereabout?'

The rider looked at him in annoyance at being mistaken for a man by a poshly dressed toff. The fourteen year old Sal Madge, for it was she, replied, not knowing who he was.

'All the land round here belongs to Lord Lowther.'

'He must have a great deal!'

'Aye the ould bugger; he has far owwer much,' said Sal and whipped up her horse to leave quickly.

The Earl of Lonsdale was over the moon with this remark which underscored his fabulous wealth. 'Young man!' he said. 'Young man, stop. Here have this.'

He was almost beside himself with his chortling and absolutely delighted with the quaintness of that which confronted him.

To Sal's amazement and pleasure he pulled a half crown piece from his fob pocket and gave it to her.

'What's this for?'

'Well, I might have owwer much, but now I've a little less and you can drink my health.'

'Oh,' said Sal, now realising who the posh bloke was, 'thou may be sure that I will.'

'I know it,' replied Lonsdale with a smile, and went on his way. After that meeting Lonsdale and Sal Madge had seen and spoken on several occasions and like John Peile before him, Lonsdale prized Sal. She was an oddity, an ornament to his possessions, like a carving by Grinling Gibbons on his wainscot or a jewel on his coronet. The anecdote of how he had met the remarkable Sal Madge was repeated at dinner many times over the years and passed down through the family as a tale worth the telling. She was the best of local colour.

The current earl knew the story off by heart and thought it a good thing that he had such a picturesque character working for him. The Yellow Earl was the nickname that people gave him for his love of the colour, and he gave himself to a life of pleasure when he came into money. His footmen wore yellow livery; his coach was the same colour and his horses wore yellow when they raced. Yellow was of course the hue favoured by his party, the Conservatives, and he was a supporter of the Primrose League whose emblem was, of course, a bright yellow primrose. He had been a keen amateur boxer, in yellow, and now he was the local earl he gave enthusiastic backing to boxing contests in the Whitehaven area, which he attended often. In his lapel he always wore a flower, which varied according to the season, but they were all of one colour. At the 1883 colliery sports he was displaying a daffodil and Sal

Madge walked up to him by the ringside of a local contest and challenged him as if he and she were equals, but by this time he knew her and answered her in kind.

'I see you like daffs; them's my favourite flower and I've a mind to win it off you. I'll wrestle thee for ten bob and thy daff. Are you game?'

'Nay Sal, I'll not wrestle you,' replied Lonsdale. 'I used to box, not wrestle and I know well that you'd throw me. I concede the match and here's the prize.'

He was laughing as he said it, delighted at the invitation and she was rewarded again, not only with the daffodil; it made him feel included and accepted in the community, which strangely, he was. The rich were often unpopular but locally people were rather fond of Lonsdale and nicknamed him 'Lordy' whilst being proud that in Whitehaven they had a proper lord who spent liberally and ostentatiously. He went away chuckling at the incongruity of the exchange. After this, it was well known that Sal had something of the license of a court jester, but in an amusing and witty way; not in any sense foolish. If the Earl of Lonsdale esteemed Sal, then Sal was worth esteeming. Edward Atter knew this truth, and so did the magistrates; she would be a formidable witness in the box for that reason alone.

It is worth noting that Sal had considerable status in town for yet another reason. She was a single woman earning a man's wage for a man's job. People were used to her doing that but for Sal it meant that she did have a certain amount of surplus income for her lifestyle. Let it not be thought that she had any large savings; she did not, for she spent a lot of it on cards and drink. Never a sot, she always had enough to pay her rent and food, but she was not a person who worshipped money. She had friends and neighbours who might fall on hard times and when that happened Sal was free with her help. She was no soft touch and would not give if asked, but she would approach people in need and give them money, never expecting it back. To someone like the Yellow Earl, the money she gave would be less than he would tip a cabman, but to those who received small amounts from her it was often the difference between food on the table and none.

She was also very forward in charitable acts, and as she grew older she donated whatever she collected by wrestling men to good causes like the Howgill Street infirmary, the lifeboat days or other organisations that took her fancy. To her mind, though she was not rich, there were many who were far worse off than she, and she had decided that whatever she could do to help, she would do; and she did, in many ways, not least in the waving of collection tins in people's faces in pubs. As may be imagined Sal Madge had considerable capital in Whitehaven, not in hard cash but in the respect and regard with which she was held and in solid goodwill.

Another way in which she had established goodwill was with the local Temperance movement, which was strange because Sal liked to drink and did not stint herself on beer. In October 1885 the growing Salvation Army movement had finally reached Whitehaven in the persons of Sarah Morton and Sarah Ann Hugill. These ladies strove to do good work in the way of their organisation, but their reception had not always been smooth. They would raise money by going into the pubs and bars, seemingly without fear, and rattling collection tins at the inebriates in these establishments, asking for money to buy soup and other things to help the needy. At the Dusty Miller their first entrance had been greeted with ribaldry and threats with some catcalling; among the loudest was John Kennedy, Sal's friend. 'Laal Piano' Bobby McKee, a man only three feet tall was playing the piano for an appreciative and drunken audience, but stopped when the strangely uniformed women came into the bar. Sal had looked at the Salvationists, considered them a moment, then rose to her feet and told Kennedy, 'Sit down thou laal radge or I'll skelp thee yan.'

Silence fell as Sal fished out a penny and put it into the collection tin. Other people followed suit and thereafter the ladies found that when they carried their campaign into enemy territory, their reception was considerably more civil. Soon, of course, they earned their own respect, but Sal had eased their path considerably. In such ways, she garnered a store of goodwill and high regard throughout the town. In addition to this, the story of how she had gone into a blazing house to pull out a poor woman who was hurt had spread round the entire district.

It was in sure regard for Sal that she was sought out by PC Thomas Beattie in her lodgings at Windmill on the afternoon of Saturday 4 June. She was not expecting any callers and especially not a policeman in plain clothes.

'This is very unexpected, Thomas. If you've come a courting I have to tell you, thou'll get nowhere fast with this'un.'

To her surprise Beattie did not grin, but kept his face solemn, as indeed his demeanour was.

'Nay Sal, I've come to tell you something I've learned, because I don't know what else to do with it. I'm not on duty because this is private twixt thee and me.'

'Oh aye? Well spit it out lad; I shall not be biting you.'

'Well you remember last February time I got attacked by a drunk down on the quay. You and John Connelly helped me out.'

'Well yis; it's nut the sort of thing you forgit. I'd have skelped him mesel if I hedn't hed yan owner t'odds. I remember the bugger got a month with hard labour and he asked for it. What about it?'

'Well that's what's bothering me you see. Connelly's in the cells accused of burning his wife and it's that same drunk and his marras that's saying he did it.'

'Is it, by God!' Sal thought for a moment. 'Thou think he's doing it out of a grudge?'

'I think so.'

'Hest thou told that superintendent of yours; what's his name? Thornburrow?'

'I did, but he says that case isn't relevant to this one. Whatever Connelly did in February does not mean that he did not do this thing in May.'

'You think this fella's making it up? What's his name again?'

'Edward Parker. Yes I do. I think there's a very good chance that's exactly what he's doing.'

'Why are you telling me?'

'I thought thou should know, since thou were there. I thought it might help.'

'Aye, well it might just do that. Tell me Thomas, is he the only witness?'

'No. There are two others. One is James Kendall and the other is Richard Walker, or so they say.'

'What? Him from Bardywell Steps?'

'The same.'

'I know them both. Kendall's a drunk; Walker is too, but not so bad. I don't know Parker though; I think he's an incomer.'

Sal Madge went deep into thought.

'Alright lad. Thank you for telling me.'

'I had thought of telling that Mr Atter too.'

'I don't think that will be necessary. I do not think Mr Atter will need any help with Parker.'

'What about the other two? Three men swearing against a man is a lot you know.'

'I know Thomas.' Sal patted Beattie's arm. 'You rest easy. You go telling owt to Mr Atter might get you in trouble with Thornburrow so don't trouble on it. Just leave the matter with me eh?'

Beattie nodded, thanked her and left, much more at ease in his mind, because Sal Madge did not say things just for the sake of it, as well he knew. When he had taken his departure, Sal filled her pipe and lit it, sat down in a tatty old armchair in the corner of her room and puffed copiously at it for about an hour. When she had sat enough and thought on things she got up and went over to her bed and lifted up the mattress. From a pouch hidden under it she took two coins. Then she went out; she did not go to her usual haunts though. Down the steps she went and threaded her way through the narrow streets to the broad quay then she headed straight for the Sun Inn on Duke Street where she knew she would find James Kendall. Sure enough he was in a corner, on his own, nursing a half pint of beer and looking miserable. He was, as she knew, not a well-liked man, being one of those who spent his wages, when he had any, on drink. He was, however, a very big strong sort of man, though weak of will. He had no wife or family so his expenditure was considerable and his aim was to stay drunk until all his cash was gone. When he had drunk a few pints he was objectionable rather than aggressive and he was not one of her normal circle of acquaintance. Nonetheless, she bought a pint of beer for herself and another for him and sat down beside him.

'You're not looking very happy, Jimmy. What's up wi thee marra eh? What fettle?'

Kendall knew Sal slightly; if he had been sober he might have hesitated and wondered why she had singled him out, but his head was muzzed and he was simply glad to talk to someone.

'Ah's nit geud Sal. Ah's nit happy. Ah've sin summat as wud mak moast folk's heear stand on't end.'

Gradually she coaxed him to talk and had the whole tale; but it was her version. He had arrived after John Kennedy and she had carried Rose Anne out of the house and the sight of the burned woman had haunted an already febrile mind into wishing to find oblivion. He had been drunk all week, but had now run out of money.

'I hear that Edward Parker is saying that he saw John Connelly holding his wife on't fire. Is that how it was?'

'It's not for me to say Sal is it? I don't know what he saw.'

'Did you see him doing that?'

'I don't think I did, but I could not swear to it.'

'I heard you telt the police.'

'Aye I know, but I telt 'em what they wanted to hear. It was Parker that saw it.'

'But you didn't?'

'Ah telt thee; I could not swear to it. I'd had a few Sal. I can't remember all that much.'

Sal Madge nodded. Kendall thought she was nodding at him, but she was nodding to herself. This man in a witness box would not be any help to John Connelly. On the other hand he might not be any harm but he was such a weak character that it was possible, if he was sober, that his words would be twisted. Big in body, he might be but soft in the head. Talking to him had confirmed what she had thought. Digging into her pocket she produced a gold sovereign and a half sovereign, part of what she had put away for a rainy day.

'Now look Jimmy, I'm sorry for thy trouble. I can see you're not a happy man right now marra, and that you might not want to go to work. I understand that, but you have to keep body and soul together. I want you to have this.'

'Really Sal? You'd help me out with that?'

'I would. A marra should always be willing to help a marra.'

'That's true Sal. That's very true.'

'There's one condition though Jimmy.'

'What's that Sal?'

'Thou's to spend it on thissen. No treating other folk and no gambling with it. It's for thou to spend on you. Promise?'

'I do Sal. I swear on my mother's grave. I'll spend it all on myself.'

Sal Madge passed over the coins, patted him on the shoulder and left; Kendall, given a week's wage for a skilled man, lurched over to the bar for another drink; he was not refused.

Her pocket slightly lighter, Sal Madge smiled grimly as she went back along the quayside heading for Bardywell Steps. She could ill afford what she had just given Kendall, but for her, friendship was more than gold. What happened next was up to Kendall, but she calculated on him doing exactly as she thought he would; he had free will after all, and he would use it. Her next visit would require slightly different tactics.

Halfway up Bardywell Steps was a door that had once been green, but was now covered in paint flakes and rot. It was ajar, so she did not bother knocking and went in. A pale and exhausted looking woman was at a table peeling potatoes; like so many, a drudge worn out by the trials of a hard life.

'I want to see thy man,' snapped Sal. 'Where is he?'

'He's in the yard.'

Mrs Walker knew very well who Sal was and did not argue.

Sal walked through the filthy front room, through an evil smelling scullery and into a dirty yard out back; there she found Richard Walker smoking a pipe. He was a thin wispy man with a threadbare ginger moustache and a permanently worried expression.

'Sal Madge! What do you want?'

He found himself fixed by a pair of dark brown eyes, hard as pebbles off the beach that seemed to look right through him.

'You're in court on Monday morning.'

'Aye that's right. I am. What about it?'

'You're going to tell the truth I hope?'

Walker was mystified.

'Yis I'll tell the truth.'

'You'll be on oath and you'll tell the truth.'

Worried now Walker said again, 'Yis; I'll tell the truth.'

Now Sal closed right up to him and stood in his space, her face right up to his, almost touching. He started to sweat; he knew her reputation. The smell of her was in his nose, not too strong, but slightly acrid, like that of an old fox.

'Understand me, Richard. You've just telt Sal Madge you'll tell the truth, eh?'

He nodded, now scared because the aggression pouring out of her was tangible, and he was not a brave man.

'Well, you make sure thou tell the truth Richard, because guess what will happen if you don't?'

'I don't knaw.'

'Not very bright are thou? I'll tell you plain; if you do not tell the truth and nowt but the truth, then you can expect a visitor the next evening. Understand?'

He gulped and nodded.

'And if that happens, Richard, you'll wish thou'd not been born.'

He was beginning to shake now and Sal grinned at him, patting his crotch.

'You's got this thing Dick, but I'm more of a man than you'll ever be. Don't make me come back.'

'I won't Sal. I won't.'

'Good lad. I'll see myself out.'

With that Sal Madge turned and walked out, giving Walker's woman a wink on the way. Different tactics suited different people and although Sal was a fair minded woman, she was most definitely not above a spot of intimidation where necessary.

At Whitehaven infirmary Rose Anne had seemed to be improving for much of the week and Dr Muriel thought that she might actually recover though she would be left horribly scarred all over her body, though her face was mercifully untouched. Dr Irwin also thought that she might beat the odds, for she was over the initial shock. Unfortunately, she developed breathing difficulties on Sunday morning and uncontrollable muscle spasms, Grimly, the doctors recognised the symptoms of tetanus and during the day it got worse. Lockjaw set in and her temperature soared into a high fever as night came on. There was nothing that they could do and the end was inevitable. On Sunday evening at about ten o'clock Rose Anne breathed her last. If her troubles were over, John Connelly's were just beginning.

A messenger to Edward Atter brought him the news as he prepared for bed and as soon as he read the message from Dr Irwin he knew that his next day's work would be one of the most important that he would have in his career. Superintendent Thornburrow was also informed and the news went round the police station. It was PC Mouatt who went down to the cells to inform the prisoner.

'Your wife just died in hospital. You'll hang for this Connelly.'

Chapter 12

Trial

Monday 6 June 1887 was a blustery day with clouds scudding low over the town, though high up was bright blue; occasional heavy flurries of rain made people scurry into shop doorways or under awnings and some hats were blown off heads as the wind channelled up Lowther Street. The weather did not deter a large crowd of people who wished to get into the public gallery of the magistrates' court. The news of Rose Anne's death had gone round the area like wildfire and, in addition to the townsfolk, there were many journalists who wished to gain entrance. Everyone knew that there would not be a murder trial; that was beyond the competence of the court; on the other hand, John Connelly would face at least one charge, and if the magistrates found that there was a case against him then he would be sent for a full murder trial at the assizes. If that happened then there would be little doubt of his guilt. The public gallery was packed out, and eventually the police had to close the door and tell the people left outside to go home. Among the people who were lucky enough to gain entrance was Sal Madge. There was some slight altercation on the door with the policeman controlling it over the propriety of admitting Flirt, but he stood no chance.

'Get away with you, Tommy. You know well enough that Flirt won't make a sound. I'll put him on my lap and he'll listen and make more sense of what's going on than most.'

'Aye Sal, you've got a point there; he's a good lad with more sense than a lot of folk. Alright, for you I'll stretch the point.'

'Thanks lad; if there's any bother about it I'll say I sneaked him in under my jacket.'

To Flirt himself she was brutally direct, 'Now, look here you little bugger. If you make a squeak in this room I'll swing you round by thy tail and throw you in't dock. You hear me?'

Flirt merely cocked an ear and panted at her; he knew very well she did not mean it.

The magistrates sitting in the bench were the same gentlemen as had done so the previous Thursday, Rev Fox presiding with Rev Dalton and Mr Fisher.

Connely had been accused of grievous bodily harm on the previous Thursday. Now he stood in the dock and Superintendent Thornburrow got up to speak.

'This man is charged with causing the death of his wife by burning her at Whitehaven on the 28th of May. On Thursday last it was reported she was doing favourably and until yesterday at noon she seemed to be going on well, but during the evening unfavourable symptoms set in and she died at the infirmary about ten o'clock last night. I am not prepared to go on with the case now, and I therefore ask for a further remand.'

Edward Atter now stood to speak and immediately raised objection to the request for remand, addressing the chairman of the bench.

'May it please your worship, I oppose this request for a further remand and I do so on the same grounds as I did last Thursday. The application to keep my client in gaol for any more time is both unreasonable and unfair. The prisoner in front of you has been in custody for over a week now and not one tittle of evidence has been adduced in front of this bench that would in any way justify his either being taken into custody or remanded.'

Reverend Fox had evidently been giving this matter some thought.

'I was going to ask for some evidence, Mr Atter. I am quite aware that some at least is required to justify a remand.'

Edward Atter pressed his advantage,

'It is true your worship that a charge is easily made. However, I must point out that as far as the bench is concerned I can see nothing whatever that justifies or supports this application for a further remand. I also see no evidence to justify this man being put upon his trial or for being detained in custody. On the contrary, as we know from the superintendent of police, the unfortunate woman made in her dying deposition a statement that her husband had nothing whatever to do with the causing of her injuries. The only actual evidence we have is such that entirely exonerates the accused. I think that unless some evidence is given then the bench must not detain this man in custody.'

Reverend Fox looked at the other two magistrates and they all nodded; what had been said was fair and reasonable. Fox looked at Superintendent Thornburrow and asked him a very blunt and direct question.

'What evidence have you to connect this man with the injuries sustained by his wife?'

Edward Atter had gone out on a legal limb by describing Mrs Connelly's statement as a dying deposition. In common law, although not binding upon the outcome of a case, a dying deposition was more often than not accepted as truth. The reasoning behind this was that in most cases, unless malice were proven, the dying person, in fear of God and the life hereafter, had no reason to lie. Such a deposition had to be sworn in front of a competent authority and in the case of Mrs Connelly that had been done. However, it had been done at a time when it was thought she might recover and a competent barrister would question its validity. If this happened then the deposition would be downgraded to a dying declaration which was considered much weaker evidence. A deposition was regarded as strong evidence and the witnesses to it could be cross examined in court; a declaration would be noted, but would not be cross examined or seen as strong.

Superintendent Thornburrow knew this, for his smooth reply immediately discounted Rose Anne's statement.

'Your worship, the dead woman made a statement in the infirmary which exonerates him, but her statement is not at all in accordance with the facts which I will be able to produce.'

Atter was having none of this. Leaping to his feet he interrupted Thornburrow.

'Then let us have these facts - or something.'

Reverend Fox agreed, 'We must have some evidence superintendent.'

Thornburrow pursed his lips and admitted, 'I have no such evidence here.'

Mr Atter was on his feet again and looking angry, 'There is such a thing as *habeas corpus*; you have no right to bring him up here for a week and give no evidence against him. You are as wise today as you were last Thursday!'

As Atter sat down, showing disgust on his face the clerk of the court, Mr Brockbank, whose job it was to advise the magistrates made a remark also.

'We really should have some evidence to justify a remand. I suggested this last Thursday and it is even more true today.'

The superintendent could see that matters were slipping out of his hands and expostulated, 'I have witnesses, but they are all over the country.'

Reverend Fox was not impressed by this statement, 'We cannot remand him unless you produce some evidence. Why did you take him into custody?'

Thornburrow had to answer this as well he knew, or Connelly would have to be freed.

'Your worship; the woman was drunk at the time she was burned. She was not drunk at the time she made her statement. May I ask that the statement be read out in court?'

Reverend Fox raised his eyebrows a little, but directed that the clerk read out Rose Anne's statement again; the courtroom was hushed as the dead woman's words rang about the room. When it was done, Superintendent Thornburrow looked around.

'You have heard the words of the statement and that the deceased set herself alight with a paraffin lamp. If it please your worship, I should like to call Dr James Irwin.'

The witness being called and sworn in, Thornburrow asked Doctor Irwin to relate what he had found when he had examined Mrs Connelly on the previous Saturday week.

'I attended the deceased at Whitehaven infirmary on Saturday night week and found her to be very severely burned. The burns extended from her heels up to her waist, the back part being more extensively burned than the front. Her buttocks and thighs were almost charred. She was in a state of extreme collapse and it seemed that she was likely to die at any moment. I advised that her deposition be taken as soon as possible.'

At this Mr Atter's left eyebrow raised slightly and he gave a wry smile, but said nothing. The doctor continued,

'Subsequently, the patient rallied. She certainly had had some drink. She was suffering from drink or shock; I could not tell which. I examined her clothes, but I have to say that I could not detect any smell of paraffin on them. Nobody could find any smell of paraffin. The front parts were not as badly burned as the back.'

Reverend Fox interpolated here, 'How could that be?'

'How it was done, I cannot say; several statements were made about the burning, but how it happened that the burns were on the back and not so much on the front I could not say.'

Edward Atter stood to ask, 'Were you present during her deposition?'

'I was not; she was, I understand, quite conscious, but I was not there. The fire must have continued for a good while to have left her in such a condition. A fire would not have exhausted the whole of the smell of the paraffin had it been on her clothes. The charred remains smelled strongly of burnt material. She made a statement that she had spilled paraffin and she also made a statement that she was working with a box of matches.'

Seeking clarification Reverend Fox asked, 'You say that she put a lamp onto the chimney piece and that some paraffin was spilled down over her dress and onto her arms. That was in her statement. Did you see that part of her dress?'

Dr Irwin nodded in affirmation, 'Yes. There was no smell of paraffin there. The paraffin would have fallen over the front part of her dress, but her back parts were the most extensively burnt.'

A murmur went round the courtroom and Mr Atter's face was unreadable. The dead woman's statement did not tally with the condition of her body or with the observations of witnesses; it began to look like a fabrication.

Superintendent Thornburrow was beginning to look like a cat with a bowl of cream and he asked leave to call Sergeant Hope, which was done. When asked to describe what he had seen, he stated that he had, on arrival at the scene, gone into the victim's house.

'The woman who had been burned was about to be put on a stretcher to be carried to the infirmary. At the time she did not seem to be conscious and only moaned a little when she was put onto the stretcher. I went into the house and made an examination of the place.'

Here the sergeant pulled out his notebook and continued his statement whilst referring to it.

'I observed a paraffin lamp on the mantelpiece. On the floor in front of the fire were some pieces of rags, and the place appeared as if water had been spilled. On the stair was a rag which struck me as signifying that the deceased woman had run upstairs a short distance. There was no smell of paraffin. The smell was that of charred rags. The lamp had not the appearance of having been moved, as shown by the dust on the mantelpiece. I have to observe though, sir, that the dust could have been caused by water being thrown onto flames; it would have that effect. When I left the house it was still quite light and the lamp was not lit. There was a bottle in the cupboard which contained some paraffin oil, and an old woman who came into the house said…'

Edward Atter sprang to his feet, 'I object if he was not present.'

'Very well, Mr Atter,' said Reverend Fox. 'You are quite right. Hearsay is not admissible as evidence.'

Atter sat down again, but any feelings of vindication he might have had were buried under the certainty that Mrs Connelly's statement had been torn to shreds.

Superintendent Thornburrow continued his questioning of Sergeant Hope,

'Sergeant, was there any wet on the mantelpiece?'

'No sir, there was not. The only wet was in front of the fire as if water had been thrown for the purpose of putting out the fire. There was a very large strong fire burning in the grate at the time.'

When Hope had finished Thornburrow, turned to the bench and looked questioningly at Reverend Fox who nodded at him. At this point a court messenger hurried from the back of the chamber and handed Fox a note. The chairman looked at it and nodded his thanks. A murmured conversation now followed between the magistrates for a couple of minutes, then Fox turned to Thornburrow again.

'We consider, Superintendent, that there is, in light of what we have heard, sufficient evidence to justify a further remand.'

Atter rose immediately, 'Until what day?'

'I shall be ready by Thursday,' replied Thornburrow.

'Well,' said Reverend Fox, 'The shorter time the better.'

'May I ask for terms of bail for my client your worship?'

'Certainly, Mr Atter. Under the circumstances we will take bail, but you must understand that it will be heavy. The prisoner must stand in £100 and there must be one surety of £100 or two separate sureties of £50 apiece.'

Atter looked at Connelly, who shook his head. He could not possibly pay or afford such an amount. He stayed in gaol.

At the end of the hearing Reverend Fox asked Edward Atter to stay behind for a few minutes with Superintendent Thornburrow.

'Gentlemen, a few minutes ago I received a note from Mr Lumb, the West Cumberland coroner. He informs me that he is convening an inquiry into the death of Mrs Connelly, which will take place in this very chamber tomorrow morning. We on the bench will attend as observers; I take it that you will also be able to do so?'

'Upon my word that is quick work!'

'Indeed so, Superintendent; Mr Lumb has been most expeditious.'

'There is no question about it,' replied Mr Atter. We must attend, I as Mr Connelly's solicitor. I imagine that there will be a notification for me at my office though I have to say it is very short notice. If you will excuse me gentlemen I must be about my business; there is a lot to do.'

Sal Madge also left the courtroom with matters on her mind. She had time to think about them and so she went to the Spirit Vaults on George Street where she ordered a gin. She did not usually drink gin, being an aficionado of the local beer, but this was a special occasion. She sniffed the single measure, tasted it, sniffed in, then downed it in one. The flame of it hit her palate and the back of her throat, and she grimaced slightly.

'Not to your taste Sal?' asked the barman.

'Not my usual tipple, George,' replied Sal, 'but welcome on this occasion thank you. What proof is this stuff?'

'Forty-five per cent,' replied the barman, squinting at the bottle.

'Strong enough for most I should think,' replied Sal.

Then she thanked George, left the pub and headed towards the harbour. On her way she went down a narrow alley between two shops that had once been large well to do houses. It was typical of these big dwellings in Whitehaven that the gardens had been built over and crammed with low cost housing and courts where rooms and tenements were low dirty and crowded full of people. One of these was an illegal shebeen, of which there were quite a few in town, despite the best efforts of the police. Here Sal bought a half pint bottle of what passed as gin in Whitehaven, if you knew where to get it; the proof was probably somewhere between sixty and ninety per cent, but nobody tested it and nobody cared; if you bought it then you purchased oblivion. This was the drink of choice of people on little or no income in Whitehaven, because a little of it went a very long way. Sal took a sip of it, grimaced and spat it out with a face of revulsion.

With this bottle stowed in an inner pocket and with Flirt in tow, Sal Madge made her way down to the harbour and perched herself on a bollard. After a couple of minutes had passed by she saw a lad she knew and called him over.

'Danny; I want you to do summat for me and if you do it you shalt have a penny.'

'What is is Sal?'

'See the corner of New Lowther Street over there?'

'Aye.'

'Well I want you to go owwer thear to the second door up on the right - Brockbanks the solicitors. You tell 'em that Sal Madge would be obliged if Mr Edward Atter could see her for a few minutes at the Lime Tongue. Here's the penny.'

'What's to stop me taking the penny and louping off with it?'

'The thick ear thou'd get from me if you did that; aye and when you least expected, you cheeky laal bugger.'

'Just asking,' replied the lad with a grin. 'I'll tell them,' and off he ran.

After a few minutes had passed by, Edward Atter appeared down the quayside, picking his way over the railway lines towards where Sal had perched herself on a bollard. As he approached her, he touched his hat and sat down on another bollard.

'I believe that we have done this before, Miss Madge.'

'Aye we have, but last time it was you sought me out. This time it's my turn.'

'Indeed, so here I am. How may I be of service to you?'

'I've got a little present for you.'

'Oh? What has occasioned this?'

'That little play I watched this morning.'

'Play?'

'Yis; in the court.'

'Oh I see. Yes I saw you there. You thought it a play?'

'I know make believe when I see it Mr Atter. Here's your present.'

'A bottle of gin. I am grateful Miss Madge and pleased at this sign of esteem, but I regret to say that I do not drink gin.'

'It's not that sort of present,' replied Sal, 'and I don't expect you to drink it. If thou did I fancy it might tek thy head off, as thou's nit the sort that's used to it.'

'Not drink it. Then what must I do with it?'

'I'll tell you shortly. First of all, Mr Atter, we must get to it in a roundabout way.'

Atter looked at her curiously, and she continued.

'When you go to church do they ever say owt about drink? I ask because I'm not, as you may gather, a churching sort of woman.'

'Yes, I would say so. The evils of drink are a regular feature in the sermons that I attend.'

'Exactly. Now as you understand it's an opinion held by a lot of people that drunkenness is something to be shamed of and if you want to be seen as respectable then you do not make a show of drinking.'

'Yes. I would say that being drunk or given to the sort of behaviour associated with drinking is to be seen as not respectable.'

'Now then Mr Atter, if that is the case there's a lot of people who are not respectable who would wish to be seen to be respectable and so that is the way they show themselves.'

'Ah Miss Madge,' said Atter, 'You put your finger on a disease of our age. There are far too many people who present a face to the world that they wish the world to believe, but underneath it does not resemble them at all. Where is all this leading?'

Sal Madge smiled slightly.

'That Doctor Irwin said that Rose Anne Connelly had been drinking.'

'True enough, though he could not tell if her condition was due to drink or shock.'

'Well Mr Atter, you'll know that she liked gin. She liked gin a lot. That's not a thing that many people would want known about; mother's ruin and all that sort of stuff.'

'Indeed not. For any woman wishing to be respectable, the knowledge that she drank gin would quickly destroy such pretensions.'

'She'd had a skinful on the day of the burning, so I'm told.'

'Certainly,' said Atter. 'I gather that she was rather addicted to it.'

Sal snorted and slipped off her bollard. She narrowed her eyes and came closer to Atter, looking him in the eyes.

'You know, for a legal man with such a reputation as you have, you're a bit slow.'

Taken rather aback, Atter asked quizzically,

'Slow?'

'Aye, slow. Don't you see it? She was a proud lass; at twenty-six she still had hopes of seeming respectable. It wasn't paraffin she spilled down her dress. She spilled summat alright, but not that.'

Atter stared at her thunderstruck.

'Oh aye Mr Atter. You've lived here twenty odd years, but you still don't know us that well. We're proud folk in Whitehaven and her pride was never going to let her admit she'd burned herself that way.'

'Gin! She spilled gin down her dress. That's why there was no odour! I am a complete dunderhead!'

'I would not go as far as that,' said Sal. 'But belike you're a bit slow sometimes, like I said. Now take that home with thee and put some in a saucer and set fire to it.'

'Why would I do that?' asked Edward Atter.'

'Call it science, Mr Atter. Call it science. That ain't pub gin; that's the proper stuff.'

Two local legends looked at each other and smiled. Mr Atter touched his hat again, thanked Sal Madge and went on his way home. When he got there he poured a small amount of the illicit gin into a saucer and set fire to it. As he watched the alcohol burned off and a lambent blue flame slowly flickered out. Left in the saucer was a small pool of liquid.

'Well I'm damned,' said Mr Atter.

There was no smell in the room.

Chapter 13

The Inquest

In the Manx Arms the air was thick with smoke and the bar was crowded with pitmen, Wednesday night or not. Down the Wellington and William pits work was as hard, dirty and dusty as on any other day, so there were always hundreds of men frequenting the many pubs and bars in the back alleys to slake their thirst. In the corner near the fire Sal held court; the game was Sal's favourite, three card Loo. It was very suited to her nature because it could, under the wrong circumstances, be extraordinarily vicious and nasty; Sal loved the cut and thrust of it, because she had been dealing with vicious and nasty all her life. She invariably triumphed. The game itself was not complicated; a group of players formed a 'pool' and each placed a sum of money in the middle of the table. Having seen the cards they were dealt, they could either abandon their cards and not play, losing their money, or elect to play. If they won the trick they stayed in the game; if they lost they had to add money to the middle. The game ended when all players had dropped out or been beaten except the winner, who took all. Sal was among friends so the stake was limited to one farthing. She had in her time been involved in some games for higher stakes and regarded an occasional foray as a useful supplement to her income. Sal was happy, for she was winning; it showed in her face.

'You's in a good mood Sal.'

'Aye. I think I am. But I'm usually in a good mood Isaac.'

'There's a lot never are around here.'

'True enough, but that's them and I'm me.'

'What makes you happy then, Sal? I've never seen you down,' observed John Kennedy.

'Eh now, that's a good question,' exclaimed Sal Madge. 'What makes me happy? Well work makes me happy, I know that.'

'You've said that often enough. You do like to graft. Why do you? A lot of people would do owt to avoid work.'

'Well again, that's them. I like to graft because that's what we were put here on this earth for. If you don't work hard then what's the point? I'd be a lazy devil just trying to avoid fending for myself. I'd rather feel that I was worth something.'

'But is that it, Sal?' asked Isaac Tyson. 'Is that all there is to it? Is that what God put us on the earth for?'

'God? I'm not sure that he's got much to do with it.'

'Do you not believe in God then, Sal?'

'Oh I know there's a god, John. I see him often enough in the weather that blows over the top of the brow or in the waves that smash over the pier. No it's not that; it's just that I think he lets us do things our own way.'

'You don't go to church though.'

'Nay I've no need of that malarkey. Protestant or Catholic; I don't give a tinker's dam about that. I think this world is ours and God lets us do as we want. If we make a mess of it then it's down to us and we're to blame.'

'Like John Connelly and his wife?'

Sal looked sternly at the speaker, 'I don't think we should speak of that. I fancy that this sorry business is not going to turn out quite as a lot of people think it is.'

'You're giving evidence tomorrow aren't you?'

'Yis Isaac I am, so if it's all the same to you that's enough talk about it. You asked me what makes me happy. Well apart from work, this does.' Here Sal indicated round the bar room with the stem of her pipe.

'What? The pub?' Isaac Tyson laughed. 'Well there's a lot would agree with you.'

'I don't mean that you nit; I mean friends.'

'Friends?'

'Aye. Just to sit here and have a pint and a game of cards with folk you like and get on with. That's what makes me happy right now. That's what life is all about.'

'You reckon?'

'I do. Friends is what makes your life worth living and without that thou's got nowt.'

'Well I reckon You've got nowt cos you've just been looed I think.'

'Damn it, I have! That's what comes of not concentrating; you kept me talking so I wouldn't notice, you bugger!'

Sal had failed to win a trick in a set of five thus lost all her stake, the mighty amount of two pennies and one farthing; she joined in the general laugh against herself.

'I made a right scrow of that! Nivver mind. It's vanya time for bed; busy day tomorrow.'

Tuesday 7 June dawned bright and fair and expectation ran high in the town as a queue formed right down Scotch Street to gain admission to the court room where Mr Lumb was to preside from 10.00am onwards. As the coroner made his entrance the chatter of the spectators hushed, for he was a very senior legal figure in the district, well known for his acerbic wit and ruthless control of his court. He had managed to assemble a full coroner's jury of eleven men and the foreman was Mr John Pickthall, a well-known house and land agent. Present also were Mr Atter, representing John Connelly; Superintendent Thornburrow had been busy. Connelly himself was present, handcuffed to a police officer, though it was not thought that he would be asked to give evidence, in view of the criminal proceedings against him. The three magistrates in charge of his case were also present. It must be noted that this was not a criminal court, so witnesses were not kept sequestered away, but sat in the main body of the courtroom until called. When they had given their testimony they would resume their places. The first witness to be called was Lizzie Jackson of number three Albion Street.

Mrs Jackson said that she kept a shop about twenty yards from the Connelly house and that Mrs Connelly sometimes dealt with her. She saw the deceased on the evening of 28 May between six and seven in the evening when she came to make a small purchase. At the time Mrs Connelly appeared to be quite well, but was not sober.

Edward Atter now asked his first question, 'Was the deceased woman, in your opinion, able to take care of herself?'

'I really could not say, sir.'

'Did she purchase drink from you very often?'

'She often came in for a little sup, sir.'

'I see. Could you tell us please what happened after she left your shop?'

'When she left she went in the direction of her house. About five or ten minutes later I saw people run in the direction of the Connelly house, so I did as well. I saw Mrs Connelly lying in the archway and there were people about her. I did not see any fire or anything of that kind.'

Asked by Superintendent Thornburrow to clarify if Mrs Connelly had required any assistance while leaving the shop, Mrs Jackson stated that she did not. Mr Atter asked if Mrs Connelly had said anything of a quarrel with her husband.

'No, sir. She made no complaint of any quarrel with her husband and I heard no noise or dispute after she left the shop.'

Mr Alfred Hooper, principal clerk to Mr Brockbank, clerk to the Whitehaven magistrates, deposed that on Monday evening, 30 May, he had accompanied Mr Dickinson to the infirmary and there saw Rose Anne Connelly. John Connelly was also present, a written notice having been served upon him, he having been charged with inflicting grievous bodily harm upon the deceased. The deceased woman had made a statement, which Mr Hooper took down in writing and now produced. Mrs Connelly's statement was then read out in court.

There was a deathly hush in the courtroom as Mr Hooper finished reading Rose Anne's statement and Mr Lumb looked at John Connelly over his glasses and said, 'I think, but I am not sure, that you put your arms up and tried to put the fire out?'

'Yes sir.'

'Very well,' said Mr Lumb looking at the jury. 'Gentlemen, bear that in mind. Mr Atter?'

'Thank you sir,' said Edward Atter, standing to ask his question.

'Mr Hooper, was the deceased woman fully conscious of what she was saying?'

'She certainly appeared so to me, sir.'

'Can you tell me how the statement was made?'

'Yes, sir. Her statement was chiefly made in answer to questions put to her. She was not pressed in any way to alter her story after her words were taken down.'

'I see. Thank you very much.'

Elizabeth Atkinson of number two Albion Street stated that Rose Anne was the second wife of John Connelly. On 28 May she had seen

Mrs Connelly about half a dozen times between two and seven o'clock.

Mr Lumb questioned her about Mrs Connelly's actions and demeanour.

'She told me she'd had a row with her husband about some money and had to send for a few pints to keep him happy.'

'How many pints?'

Here Mrs Atkinson hesitated, then replied tentatively, 'Three or four sir.'

'And what happened next?'

'About half past seven my little girl told me that the Connelly's house was on fire. I went to the house and I saw Rose Anne lying across the fireside. All the clothes were burned off her legs and the flames were burning on her chest. She was lying on her left side with her head towards the door. She appeared as if she were asleep and did not stir until the young men who went into the house removed her.'

'Did you see Mr Connelly?'

'No, sir. I saw nothing of him; the house was full of smoke.'

'Did the deceased woman say anything?'

'No, sir. Not a sound, at least not until they got her outside when she shouted as if she were hurt. She did not make any noise before that.'

'Did she complain of anyone?'

'No sir, she did not complain of anyone at all.'

'Can you say how she got burned?'

'No sir, I cannot.'

Edward Atter now rose to his feet with a question he had been turning over and over in his head for some hours.

'Can you think why Mrs Connelly was found lying in such an odd position in front of the fire?'

Mrs Atkinson hesitated a moment.

'Well sir, she was in the habit of tending to the fire whilst sitting on the fender. I have seen her doing it and have been told it was her habit.'

Once again a murmur went around the room, quelled by a sweeping gaze from Mr Lumb.

'And can you remember what she was wearing that day?'

'Yes sir; she was wearing a light winsey dress.'

'A material of cotton and wool, such as would readily take flame?'
'Yes sir.'

Questioned again by Mr Lumb about whether or not Mr Connelly had said anything, she replied, 'I was close by when the prisoner was taken into custody sir, and he was showing the young men where his hands were burned, but I could not tell what he was saying.'

Mr Lumb thanked Mrs Atkinson and she was allowed to leave the stand. The next person to take the oath was Edward Parker. He was stone cold sober and had a slight smile on his face as if he was going to enjoy what was to follow. Mr Lumb asked him to say what he had seen when he arrived at the fire.

'Well your honour…'

'I have not that distinction Mr Parker. You must address me as Mr Lumb, or sir.'

'Oh, yes, sir,' replied Parker, not looking quite so sure of himself.

'Well, I was with Richard Walker and John Kendall on that day when someone came and told us about the fire. So we ran to Connelly's house. We looked in and saw Mrs Connelly lying on the fire and John Connelly by the door.'

'Did he say anything?'

'Yes sir. He said "What do you want here? You have no business here." I said "There's a fire in the house. Where is it?" Then Connelly gave me a shove.'

'A shove you say. What did you do then?'

'I shoved him back sir and James Kendall buckled him one.'

'Buckled?' asked Mr Lumb.

'I believe sir that he means that Kendall struck Mr Connelly in the stomach and he folded over,' suggested Edward Atter.'

'I see. Please continue Mr Parker.'

'Anyway the woman was got out and I went up and the child was lying on the floor. I carried her out. The woman was still burning when she was carried out. Connelly was still standing by the door, but I could not say if he were drunk or sober sir. He did not give us any assistance and seemed vexed at us going into the house.'

Mr Atter's face was a mask of scepticism and he murmured to John Connelly, 'Say nothing but leave all to me.'

The coroner's face was showing open disbelief as he asked his next question.

'Do you mean to say, to tell us calmly, he saw her burning and took no notice?'

'Yes sir,' replied Parker. An audible gasp swept the courtroom.

'He was standing straight up. His legs were very nearly touching her head where she was lying.'

This was almost too much for Atter who rolled his eyes, whispering to himself, 'From where he was standing by the door to where she was lying by the fire…'

Parker continued his lurid tale as if reading from a penny dreadful.

'Her legs were under the fire grate and her clothes were burning. She did not scream or squeak. I was present when the police took Connelly away. We gave him in charge.'

'Who gave him in charge?' asked Mr Lumb.

'Me and Walker and Kendall.'

'What for?'

'What for? Because there was nobody in the house.'

'Why did you give him in charge?'

'Because he was standing close by her and we did not see him doing anything about it. And when I was bringing the child downstairs Connelly grabbed her by the neck and I had to shove him against the boiler to get him off. Another chap hit him one.'

By this time there were many faces in the courtroom beginning to register doubt. Parker did not present a very heroic figure to be cast in the story he was telling. The coroner was curious about Connelly's apparent inaction.

He might have thought you were running off with the child I suppose. You tell us on your oath that he stood when this woman was burning under the grate and he took no notice?'

'He didn't look as if he was taking any notice.'

Mr Atter stood up, 'You say that when you arrived Mr Connelly's clothes were on fire in front?'

'Yes, that's right.'

'You did not extinguish them? When was that done?'

'He was taken into the house to put it out when the police arrived.'

'I see,' said Edward Atter, lifting his eyebrows at the jury.

'Tell me, Mr Parker, did you notice any damp on the stairs?'
'No, the stairs were not damp.'
'Thank you,' said Mr Atter and sat down, shaking his head.

'Call Sarah Madge,' said the coroner and there was some chatter as the well-known figure made her way to the stand and was sworn in with her hand on the bible. Sarah Madge, single woman of Whitehaven swore to tell the truth, the whole truth and nothing but the truth. She stood there, a commanding figure and as all knew, one that held her own in the world. Perhaps never in her life had she looked so dignified as standing in front of the coroner about to give her testimony. Had it crossed the minds of the people in the court, she might have been some ancient queen surveying her own court before delivering judgment. Invited by Mr Lumb to tell what she had seen on the evening of 28 May, she began,

'John Kennedy and myself arrived at the house and there was smoke coming out of the door. We did not see Mr Connelly at all, but we could see the woman lying on the fire. John Kennedy and myself carried her out. We couldn't stay long in the house, because of the stife. The woman was actually frizzling when we were carrying her.'

'Did you speak to Mrs Connelly at all?'

'Aye. I said to her, "This is terrible; how did it happen?" She didn't say owt though. I think she was insensible.'

'Did you see Mr Edward Parker?'

'Nay. I saw nowt of him until he came up after with the stretcher.'

Mr Atter now stood to question Sal.

'May I ask, did you notice the smell of paraffin in the house?'

'There was no smell of paraffin in the house.'

Once again there was a murmur in the courtroom.

'Are you certain that it was yourself and Mr Kennedy who were first into the house?'

'As certain as I stand here. John Kennedy and myself were the first into the house and it was us as carried her out.'

'My apologies for repeating this question, but I have to be quite clear. You did not see Edward Parker in the house?'

'Parker was not in the house; only John Kennedy and myself.'

'Parker did not assist you in any way?'

The full attention of the entire courtroom was on Sal Madge as she glanced round the chamber and said firmly, 'Parker did not assist us in any way.'

It was as if a cloud had lifted. This was Sal Madge speaking, and if what she said was true then Parker's testimony had to be nothing more than a pack of lies.

Mr Atter was trying to stifle his jubilation, but without success. Making a few notes in his book for the criminal case which would have to be played out, he light heartedly asked Sal, 'May I put down Mrs or Miss?'

The court erupted with laughter, as did Sal, and it was as if a boil had been lanced.

'That will be Miss,' she replied, her eyes creasing at the corners.

Mr Lumb, who knew perfectly well who she was, decided to add to the fun.

'You are a single woman I suppose?'

Sal elected to reply with a single word, 'Yis.'

The coroner smiled and a ripple of amusement went round the chamber.

On her way back to her seat Sal passed the next witness, Richard Walker. She gave him a meaningful look, which he saw quite clearly, but it was not needed. His mind was already made up. He stood in the witness box. He and Parker had gone to the Connelly house on being told there was a fire. They rushed in and Walker himself ran upstairs to bring out the child. The stairway was full of old bits of cloth which were smoking. He saw the dead woman frying on the fire and it was something scandalous to see and he hoped that he might never see anything like it again.

At this point the faces of the jury were a sight to see for expressions of open-mouthed disbelief. They were being asked to believe that this man had run straight past a woman burning to death on a fire and gone upstairs in her house. It was too much, but the charade had to play out to its end as Walker continued. Connelly was standing by the door with his arms folded and it seemed to Walker that he might have had a fit of the horrors from the night before by drinking too much.'

The coroner asked Walker, 'Had you been drinking?'

'Yes, sir. I had two pints of ale in the Dusty Miller and it put me in good heart to go into the house and get the woman out.'

It was not a murmur, but a buzz of disbelief that went round the room now.

'Her clothes had been burned off and a man took off his coat to cover her limbs.'

This was too much for the jury and one of its members asked permission to put a question to the witness. Mr Lumb assented.

'Did you see Sarah Madge there?'

Walker's face registered a slight uncertainty, but he answered as if by rote. 'Yes. We were there about twenty minutes before her. We went to the house between seven and eight o'clock.'

At this, another juryman could not restrain himself but said out aloud, 'That's a puzzler.'

'Quiet please,' said Mr Lumb. 'Mr Atter?'

'Thank you, sir. Mr Walker; you say you had drunk two pints of beer? Is that all you had?'

Walker looked weedy and unsure of himself, shuffling his feet.

'Well sir, I think I had four.'

'Oh, four, not two. And your companions also?'

'Yes sir; we had all drunk four.'

'You said two, but now admit to four?'

'Yes, sir.'

'And you swear that Mrs Connelly was carried out as you say?'

'Yes, sir.'

The coroner now asked Walker what had happened when the police arrived.

'When the policeman came he put the bracelets on Connelly. I gave him orders to do it, because he had seen that woman lying in such a state and done nothing about it and that was my reason. Such a sight would make anyone do something, but he was looking on as daft as a yat.'

If this was an attempt at humour it fell on deaf ears; nobody smiled or laughed. Walker shuffled his feet some more, but Atter had had enough. Mr Lumb told Walker to stand down and called PC Mouatt. His first question was very to the point.

'Constable; why did you arrest Mr Connelly?'

'Well sir, because the last witness told me that he had put his wife on the fire.'

Mr Lumb nodded and then turned his attention to where Richard Walker was sitting.

'Why did you tell the policeman that?'

Sal Madge was looking at Walker and he knew it.

'I said nothing of the kind, sir.'

The courtroom erupted with gasps of disbelief.

'Quiet! Quiet!' insisted the coroner. 'I see. Constable, please continue and tell me what happened when you arrived at the scene of the fire.'

'Well sir, I saw Mrs Connelly lying outside and I took Mr Connelly into custody. He said his hands were burned and his trousers were burning and the fire was put out. Mr Walker said that Connelly had put his wife on the fire, so I asked him if he had. He said nothing. He was under the influence of drink, sir.'

'Did he seem as if he had been pushed out of the way?'

'No sir, he did not.'

'Was the floor of the house wet?'

'Yes it was.'

'Did you smell paraffin at all?'

'No, sir. Not a trace of it.'

'And was the fire in the grate large or small?'

'Large sir; a good big one.'

'What made the last witness tell you that Connelly had put her on the fire; do you know?'

'I don't know, sir.'

'About what time was this?'

'I am sure it was about twenty minutes to eight when Walker told me about the matter'

'Very well. Mr Atter?'

'Would you say, Constable, that Mr Walker was drunk?'

'Oh very drunk, sir.'

'Was there a single man amongst them who was sober?'

'Yes, sir. Parker appeared to be, but the others were under the influence of drink.'

'And how do you know it was twenty minutes to eight?'

148

'Although Walker told me that Connelly had put his wife on the fire I was calm enough to look at the clock.'

'Thank you Constable,' said Mr Lumb, fishing out his watch. I see that it is now one o'clock and I imagine that most people will be feeling the need for sustenance. We shall adjourn until half past two.'

Some people left the room; many did not. They did not wish to lose their seats and would stay out the time. Several sets of testimony had been given each contradicting the other; but who was telling the truth?

Chapter 14

A Verdict

In Cumbrian dialect, as Edward Atter well knew, an 'atter' is a spider. As he sat taking a light lunch in the Black Lion in King Street, he reflected that he felt much like a spider, sitting in its web and waiting to catch a fly. Actually, the fly was pretty well caught, for Atter was lunching with the coroner, whom he knew well. Lumb had been a very distinguished local solicitor before becoming the coroner; he had his eye on Atter and an idea that he would wish to groom the younger man as his successor, for he was getting very much on in years. Mr Lumb believed in eating heartily; none of your 'light lunches' for him. As he wolfed down his meat and two veg he was expostulatory about what he had just heard.

'I have to say, young Edward, that the whole thing looks absurd.'

'Oh, I have to agree, sir. A pack of drunks accuse a man of murdering his wife by holding her onto a fire and an over zealous constable arrests the man.'

'Yes, yes. I have no power of course to bring in such a verdict and were this a criminal case we should not be even talking about it, but I ask you!'

'The whole thing is ridiculous. Well the magistrates have been attending as witnesses. Let us hope that they see the sheer stupidity of it all.'

'Indeed; Sal Madge for all love! They contradict Sal Madge, Edward.'

'Why man, she doth bestride this narrow world like a colossus!'

'Well, quite. She is a strange one, is she not?' Mr Lumb chortled. 'I do appreciate the reference Edward, but I cannot see her in any shape or form as Caesar's wife; perhaps more akin to Caesar?'

'Oh agreed; she is no beauty, but for my money integrity shines out of her every pore.'

'I do not disagree. I may not find one way or another, but I fancy that the people in the court are making up their own minds.'

'It will have a bearing on Thursday.'

'Of course. If it were down to me I'd release the man straight away.'

'Oh, I think we are not quite out of the trees yet.'

Lumb looked at Atter shrewdly, 'You mean the paraffin.'

'Yes. She swore that she spilled paraffin. There is still a chance that the wretched stuff could hang her husband.'

'Do you intend to speak about it this afternoon?'

' I think not. I intend to hold it in reserve for another occasion, but I fancy that the outcome of today will not be displeasing to me; or to my client.'

'I imagine that will be the case, but the paraffin has the potential to discredit the wretched woman's statement. If it does then there are still questions about how she ended up on the fire.'

'I know it sir, but if that tale stands then the whole thing must go to the assizes and Connelly's life will be on trial.'

'Oh, if it does I think their worships the magistrates should look a bunch of flats to send a man to trial for his life on such a flimsy charge sheet.'

'I agree; but it is still possible.'

Mr Lumb glanced at Mr Atter with a deadpan face, 'I shall do what I can this afternoon; we do not wish that any aspect of law in Whitehaven should be thrown into such a disgrace; the people at the assizes will think us numbskulls otherwise. But due process Edward; due process!'

Mr Lumb resumed the proceedings in the afternoon by recalling Richard Walker, who now came to the witness stand looking very unsure of himself. The coroner was not in a mood to stand on ceremony and asked him bluntly,

'Mr Walker; are you absolutely positive that you did not tell PC Mouatt that Mr Connelly had put his wife on the fire?'

'I am completely positive, sir; I did not say that to the policeman.'

'Then how does the constable know that Mr Connelly put his wife on the fire?'

'I think it was just the policeman's own idea, sir, and it ran away with him.'

'I see. Have you anything else to add that might help us here?'

'Well when the woman was taken outside I asked Connelly why he had not taken her outside or put a sheet on her and he never replied.'

'Thank you; you may sit down.'

At this point, one of the jurymen made a statement. He felt that the witness Kendall should be present to give evidence. The coroner agreed.

'Mr Thornburrow; can you account for the absence of such a vital witness?'

'Yes sir,' replied the superintendent. 'He has been in a state of complete beastly drunkenness since the fire, such that he is not fit to appear. The same is true of John Kennedy.'

'Where on earth do they find the money?' wondered the coroner. 'No matter - we must proceed with what we have. I should like to question Sergeant Hope.'

Hope's testimony agreed with that of PC Mouatt until it came to a point just before the arrest of Connelly.

'I saw Parker, who said that the man of this house had put his wife on the fire and held her there until a young fellow had rushed in and throttled him. He said that he and four others had been in the house, but who the man was that throttled the husband I have not been able to learn.'

'Because he didn't exist,' came a voice from the back of the court.

'Be quiet sir!' snapped Mr Lumb. 'You will disregard that Sergeant. Please continue.'

'I spoke to the man Kennedy; he was clearly drunk.'

'Do you mean Kennedy Sergeant, or was it Kendall?'

'I beg your pardon sir; it was Kendall. He would do nothing, but insist that I pay him to carry the woman to the infirmary.'

Mr Lumb nodded, 'Have you any ground or evidence for saying, either by yourself or others that this man actually put his wife on the fire or caused her to be burned?'

Sergeant Hope swallowed hard, aware of his superintendent's eye fixed upon him, but he pulled himself together and answered manfully,

'I have not. There are only certain circumstances.'

'You charged him nonetheless.'

'I did sir. The prisoner, when charged, replied that he did not know why it had happened and also that he had put out his hands to extinguish the flames.'

A noise of sympathy ran round the room; Mr Atter heard it and sensed that the mood had changed, no matter what the newspapers had been saying about Connelly.

The sergeant continued, 'The prisoner was visited by his daughter in the cells on the Sunday following the fire. He told her that he did not know how it occurred at all. He had just gone into a sleep on the side of the fire and he wakened and saw her in flames. She ran upstairs, but he got hold of her and pulled her down. He got a bucket of water and tried to put out the fire. He got his arms burnt and then a lot of drunken fellows ran in and abused him. The prisoner was sober at the time he said this sir.'

'The house was wet?' asked Edward Atter.

'Yes, sir. It was.'

Sal Madge was recalled to the stand and as she looked about her, her glance was like a fury unleashed and her scorn plain for all to see.'

The coroner was brief.

'Miss Madge, I regret I must ask you again. How was Mrs Connelly got out of the house?'

'John Kennedy and myself got Mrs Connelly out of the house. There was no one else. After we had done it Parker and Walker came up and made a load of fuss about policemen and stretchers.'

She stood like a rock and truth shone out of her enough to hush the room.

'Thank you, Miss Madge. Call Rose Ann McCumisky.'

Nurse McCumisky took the stand and stated that she was a nurse at Whitehaven infirmary.

'Can you tell me please what the deceased, Mrs Connelly, said about how she came to be set on fire?'

'Yes, sir. Mrs Connelly told me that the oil fell down from the lamp and set her on fire. Her husband had nothing to do with it. She actually told me that several times. Mrs Connelly told me that she dreaded the ninth day and that if she was going to die she would make a will to say that her husband had nothing to do with it.'

'The ninth day?' asked the coroner.

'If a burns victim is going to develop an infection sir then it usually appears on the ninth day after the fire.'

'Thank you, nurse. You may step down now. Call Doctor Irwin.'

Doctor Irwin gave evidence that the cause of death was tetanus, due to infection taking root in the very severe burns suffered by Mrs Connelly. He was supported in this by Dr Harris, the house surgeon from the infirmary, and Dr Jackson, the visiting surgeon. This completed the tally of the witnesses and Mr Lumb was able to proceed with his summing up to the jury.

'Gentlemen of the jury; this is a serious case. The circumstances are of very great suspicion and they require serious consideration at your hands. It is one of those cases that arise from the effects of drink. It is beyond doubt that the wife was drunk. The husband appears to have had something to drink, but he does appear to have known what he was doing. If the husband put his wife on the fire and allowed her to burn, then there never was a worse case of wilful murder. If you think this is a case of wilful murder, then you should say so. I must emphasise that in this case you may not return a verdict of manslaughter. It is indeed a very suspicious case, but I must point out that Mrs Connelly did exonerate her husband and that she did this not once, but several times. She also did it under oath and in front of a justice of the peace. Please consider well of your verdict.'

The jury retired and was out only about five minutes before they returned. The corner looked at them enquiringly, 'Have you reached a verdict?'

'We have, sir.'

'What is your verdict?'

Mr Pickthall, the jury foreman stood up and announced in a loud voice, 'We find that death was caused by tetanus produced by burns. How those burns were caused, there is not enough evidence to satisfy the jury.'

'Thank you, Mr Foreman. Mr Clerk, let the verdict be recorded so for the burns, but upon the circumstances please record "open verdict". This hearing is closed.'

The spectators now left the court in flurries of excited chatter and the word spread like wildfire throughout the town that the infamous wife burning case was probably not as dastardly as had been made out in the newspapers. There was, however, a lot of speculation upon the subject of paraffin; that was also the centre of Edward Atter's thoughts as he approached Superintendent Thornburrow, and all three of the observing magistrates, Reverend Fox, Reverend Dalton and Mr Fisher.

'Gentlemen, I am obliged to you for waiting, as I know you have appointments, but I think it would be a good thing for us to have a conference at this point. I do not mean at this very minute, but if it is convenient for you to wait upon me at ten o'clock tomorrow morning, there is a point of evidence which we must discuss and it is better done before we convene the court in this case.

The four men pulled out their diaries.

'It's all very well Mr Atter, but I have engaged to have coffee with the ladies' knitting circle.'

'I understand that there may be inconvenience Reverend, but the matter is rather a serious one concerning paraffin.'

'Paraffin? Indeed? Oh very well; I shall tell Mrs Dalton that she must go in my stead.'

The following morning, coffee was served in the largest meeting room upstairs in the offices of James Brockbank & associates in New Lowther Street. It was a space well appointed for its purpose, possessing a table, dark wood panelling on the walls and a number of studded green leather armchairs. It was Reverend Fox who opened the discussion, looking at Edward Atter intently.

'I have to observe young man that these proceedings are highly irregular, but I assume that you are well aware of that already.'

'I am sir, and I am grateful to you for the confidence you have in my proceeding in this manner.'

'If I did not, then you may be assured that I would not be here. You wish to speak to us of paraffin.'

'Yes, I do.'

Superintendent Thornburrow interjected, 'Mr Atter, you cannot deny that there is a discrepancy between Mrs Connelly's sworn statement and the facts. There was no smell of paraffin in the house or upon the victim and several witnesses have attested to that.'

'Indeed Superintendent, and I do not dispute it.'

'Then why do you wish to speak of paraffin?'

'Because of its absence.'

'That is rather enigmatic Mr Atter,' said Reverend Dalton.

'My apologies, sir. I do not mean to be. The relevant fact is that I concede the point completely. There was no paraffin.'

'So the woman lied in her statement,' cried out Thornburrow. 'If she lied about one thing, then why should we believe a word of the rest of it?'

'I see your point Superintendent, but I wish us to agree to rule out the mention of paraffin in evidence during tomorrow's proceedings.'

'Why on earth should I agree to such a thing? It is the strongest indication that the statement exonerating your client is false!'

'Indeed it is, but I hope to persuade you that paraffin as evidence here is inappropriate.'

'Inappropriate?' said Mr Fisher.

'Yes, sir. You see I believe I know what happened in that room.'

'Then please enlighten us, Mr Atter.'

'You will recall that the paraffin lamp, contrary to what Mrs Connelly said, was in its place on the mantelpiece and according to Sergeant Hope it was undisturbed.'

'True enough.'

'There was some paraffin in a bottle, but it was in a cupboard. If she had been attempting to refill the lamp, it would not have been.'

'Also true, but her husband said that she was attempting to refill the lamp.'

'Indeed he did, but unfortunately he was present at the hospital when the statement was given; he was restating what his wife said.'

'So you think the assertion that she was trying to refill the lamp is false?'

'I do, but please, allow me to explain. You will recall that the day was warm, yet witnesses state that there was a big strong fire in the grate, far larger than would be needed for cooking in the normal run of things. So why was the fire so big gentlemen?'

Mr Atter had all their attention now.

'Mrs Connelly was wearing a light winsey dress. She was in the habit of perching on the fender. We heard that from a neighbour.'

Edward Atter looked round; he had their agreement for there were nods.

'It was a fine day and quite warm. The fire was needed for cooking it is true, but it was apparently far bigger than was necessary on such a day. If such a large fire was not necessary then how did it get that way?'

By now his audience were looking puzzled.

'Why do you tend a fire?'

'Well, if you don't,' ventured Superintendent Thornburrow, 'then it may go out.'

'Exactly so,' replied Mr Atter. 'So coal was put on the fire. Would this always have the effect of reviving it?'

'Not if it was almost out,' said Reverend Dalton.

'Well, now we reach the question,' said Mr Atter. 'What do some people do if a fire is almost out and they wish to revive it?'

'Well it might be best practice,' said Reverend Fox 'to rake it out and allow it to burn up with some small coals or even wood.'

'Yes indeed; that is what many people would do; but what if they were in a hurry, or drunk and could not be bothered to go to all that trouble?'

'Well they might use an accelerant,' said Mr Fisher.

Edward Atter smiled. 'Paraffin?'

'We are back to paraffin,' said Reverend Fox. 'I thought we had ruled it out.'

'So we have,' said Mr Atter.

Mr Fisher was quicker than most. 'You imply the use of another accelerant?'

'I do.'

'Oh, come now, sir,' expostulated Superintendent Thornburrow. 'There is no evidence of that.'

'Indeed not; no more than there is of paraffin.'

'Then what do you think was used?'

'Gin Superintendent. High proof and very volatile gin.'

Thornburrow's face was a picture of astonishment.

'Why do you say that, Mr Atter?'

'Several reasons Superintendent. Firstly the dead woman said she spilled something down her dress.'

'She said paraffin!'

'She did; but I believe it was a euphemism.'

Thornburrow's vocabulary did not stretch to this and his brow furrowed. Seeing his puzzlement Mr Fisher explained.

'She used one word Superintendent but she really meant another.'

'But why would she do such a thing?' asked Reverend Fox.

Mr Atter looked at him, 'Because of the stigma sir. She aspired to appear respectable. To make a statement in front of a JP saying that she had been beastly drunk and that she had burned herself by throwing gin on the fire to revive it would give her a name that she did not wish to have. She would have been looked down on as a drunken woman; a slut who spent money on gin. One who had brought her own misfortunes on her head through sottishness. It is not a good reputation to wish upon oneself.'

'No indeed,' mused Mr Fisher. 'So what do you think happened in the room?'

'I believe it was an accident. She had probably formed the habit of reviving the fire with a little paraffin. It would be a careless habit because paraffin gas can explode, but much of the time she could have got away with it.'

'Why did she not this time?'

'Laziness Superintendent. She was drunk and holding a tumbler of gin. She perched herself as usual on the front of the fender and poked the fire. When it became apparent that it was going out she could not be bothered to get up to fetch paraffin, small coals or wood. She simply put more coal on; this had no effect. Then what appeared a good idea occurred to her. Twisting slightly, probably to her left, she threw the remainder of a tumbler of illegal gin onto the fire.'

'My God; it must have flared up like a veritable inferno! It must have enveloped her entirely!'

'Yes Reverend, I think it must. Spirit thrown onto flames reacts in a very different way to paraffin. Taken utterly by surprise, she was completely caught in the flames, leaped to her feet in alarm and her clothes took fire at the rear.'

'That explains why the flames burned her far more on the back than the front.'

'Quite. She panicked and ran towards the stairs; why, I cannot tell. Her husband, almost catatonic from drink, was shocked into trying to do something and threw some water over her. He attempted to beat out the flames with his hands and got burned himself in the process; she collapsed by the fire. I might add gentlemen that some water is left behind when high proof illegal gin is burned which would add to the wet on the floor.'

'And of course,' said Reverend Fox, 'that would explain the size of the fire when the constable arrived.'

'That was my thought also.'

'But why are you telling us this now Atter? Why not bring the matter out in court tomorrow.'

'Ah now, that is why I asked you here gentlemen, for we are all gentlemen are we not?'

The other men exchanged puzzled looks.

'You see, the poor woman was in fear of the ninth day as we were informed by the nurse who tended her; she knew she might die, yet she lied in her statement by saying that she spilled paraffin. I believe it was gin that was the cause of her injuries. She was trying to save what was left of her reputation gentlemen and her husband backed up what she said in loyalty to her good name. He did not wish her to appear a drunk. Think of it. In what was in effect a dying declaration, she did what she could to salvage her good name. You are here so that I may appeal to your sense of decency and what is appropriate; *De mortuis nil nisi bonum*. I am of a mind to honour her wishes. If we set the paraffin aside and test the case against my client solely on the witness evidence, then I will be content. Otherwise, to save her husband I must drag her through the mud.'

Superintendent Thornburrow was looking puzzled, for he had no Latin; Reverend Dalton observed his expression.

'"*Of the dead speak nought but good*" Superintendent. You have cast sufficient doubt in my mind Atter, I do confess, but your appeal is to our chivalry?'

'Not entirely. You must add to it the fact that gin when burned leaves no smell and then ask whether the testimony of Walker and Parker or the testimony of Sal Madge is going to stand up in court tomorrow.'

'You are banking on Sal Madge's testimony being more credible than that of Walker's or Parker'?' asked Mr Fisher.

'I'm happy for the bench to decide on that matter sir.'

159

'She has a name for honesty and hard work that would be difficult to improve upon,' mused Reverend Dalton. 'I am full of years enough to remember old Peile; he thought very highly of her. As indeed have all her employers as far as I can gather; Lonsdale does. If this case were clearer I have an idea that we should be recommending her for some kind of award for saving life.'

'Well yes,' exclaimed Mr Fisher. 'How many people, let alone any woman, would rush into a burning house to drag out a victim from the flames? It was a most extraordinary thing; astonishing courage.'

'I agree,' said Reverend Dalton. 'To walk into a house from which smoke is billowing and apparently with no thought of her own safety; well it was an admirable thing. And to do so with no other intention than to save life at the considerable risk of her own; that is pure valour Edward, and of the highest order too in that it was a completely unselfish act. One might almost say that it was an absolute good.'

'I have to say that it is quite in accord with what I have heard of her character,' said Edward Atter, 'but the testimony of the drunken men throws such doubt onto it that any thought of an award would be still born.'

'Well,' said Reverend Fox. 'You have produced enough doubt in my mind also with your theory, so unless it can be proven in court that Connelly actually held his wife on the fire, I see no reason to blacken this poor woman's name any further than it has been. Superintendent?'

Thornburrow's face was working hard and expressions chased each other across it.

'There is something else Superintendent,' said Mr Atter. 'We are supposed to send to the assizes those cases where there is a reasonable prosecution to be made against an accused. The learned judges are not amused by what they see as frivolous or baseless cases. The question of paraffin or gin is really not very relevant. The key question is can it be proven that my client held his wife onto the fire? If the court decides tomorrow one way or another on that matter, then I shall be quite content.'

'Thornburrow remembered the case of Patrick France, saw the sense of this, and nodded, 'Very well, sir. We shall concentrate on the alleged crime and disregard the paraffin.'

'I think that right,' said Mr Atter. 'It is a red herring which draws us away from the allegation that a dreadful crime has been committed. Let us see what the morrow brings and whose testimony will stand up best in a criminal court under oath.'

The other magistrates, agreeing that the paraffin would not be examined as evidence, now broke up and went about their days. Mr Atter drew in a deep breath after their departure and poured himself a brandy; he felt he had earned it.

Chapter 15

A Magisterial Decision

During Wednesday evening Mr Fisher, one of Whitehaven's team of magistrates, was taken ill, and consequently was unable to appear in court on the Thursday. Happily Mr Dickinson, another of the team had been at the coroner's court observing and thus was fully in possession of all that had transpired at that hearing. Reverend Bolton was also indisposed and was replaced by Mr Jefferson, a very experienced man, but Reverend Fox still presided in the chair. Superintendent Thornburrow opened proceedings by stating that there had been a coroner's inquest into the death of Mrs Connelly that had returned an open verdict, but that it was his task to place the evidence before the magistrates so that they could decide what would happen. Once again, the courtroom was packed out, but this being a criminal court, witnesses were not in the room.

The facts presented were much as had been given to the coroner. Edward Parker retold his story about John Connelly shoving him; he and the chaps with him carried the woman out from where they found her burning under the grate. It was he who went upstairs and brought the child out. When Edward Atter stood to question him, his face took on a guarded expression.

'Mr Parker, you are not unfamiliar with this courtroom are you?'

'No sir; I have been here on many occasions.'

'Why is that so?'

'Because I have been charged with offences many a time.'

'Have you ever been in gaol?'

The interest in the courtroom was intense.

'Yes, I have.'

'Thank you; no more questions.'

'Step down Parker,' said Reverend Fox. 'Call Sarah Madge.'

Edward Atter asked her again the very simple question that she had answered before.

'Who carried Mrs Connelly out of the house?'

'It was John Kennedy and myself; no one else.'

Once again a murmur rippled round the chamber.

'Did you see Edward Parker in the house at all?'

'Nay; he came slavering up afterwards and made a great row about it.'

'You are certain that it was after you had carried the woman out?'

'Yes; he came up after the woman had been carried outside.'

'To be quite clear, I ask again. Did you see Edward Parker in the house at any time?'

'I did not.'

This time the voices could not be restrained. Excited conversation broke out right across the courtroom, which caused Reverend Fox to bang his gavel and demand silence.

'This is a court of law and silence will be maintained. Anyone who cannot hold their tongue shall be removed by the officers of the court!'

This admonition had its effect and all was quiet once more. Edward Atter asked one more question.

'Was Parker drunk or sober.'

Sal Madge looked at him, then at the court, and then at Reverend Fox before stating pithily, 'Well if he wasn't drunk he was daft!'

That did it. Despite the chairman slamming his gavel repeatedly on his desk, the courtroom dissolved into guffaws of laughter. Sal's face remained deadpan, but her eyes twinkled at the effect of her words. The audience knew whom to believe.

Richard Walker was called next, but his story had changed slightly. On Tuesday he had rushed into the house, past the burning woman and run upstairs to get the child out of the house. Today, he stated that it was Parker who had brought the woman out first and then gone back for the child. Questioned by Mr Atter, he also admitted that he too was familiar with the courtroom and had been in gaol on a number of occasions. Some of the people in the courtroom had attended the coroner's inquest also and now there was a lot of whispered disbelief and rolling of eyes.

PC Mouatt and Sergeant Hope repeated the evidence they had given to the coroner and Mouatt again stated that Walker was drunk when he said that Connelly had put his wife on the fire. Hope, however, added to his statement,

'I have been told by several people that there was a fourth man in the house apart from Parker, Walker and Kendall, but we have been unable to trace who it was.'

'Where is Kendall?' asked Reverend Fox.

'Still drunk, sir.'

'Still? He is quite a sot! Kennedy too I imagine? Mr Atter?'

'Thank you your worship; I believe that is so. Sergeant, I recall we had a case at Carlisle not long ago where there was also a "fourth man" and he also could not be traced.'

The sergeant ruminated on this for a moment or two before replying in a rather lugubrious manner.

'I cannot learn that there was a fourth man. I am satisfied that the fourth man was really Sal Madge.'

Edward Atter could not restrain his glee, 'That cannot be, you know. Sarah Madge is a woman.'

The court erupted. When the laughter had been quashed there was a grave hush as Rose Anne Connelly's statement was read out once more to a court. Following this, Dr Irwin gave evidence as to the cause of death; at no point in the proceedings was paraffin mentioned. When the doctor was done and various onlookers had been called and answered questions in their turn, the whole sorry tale had played itself out on the legal stage and it was time to bring matters to a close. Was John Connelly to be sent to Carlisle to stand trial for his life, charged with the brutal and atrocious murder of his wife, or was he not? Mr Edward Atter rose to speak and addressed the bench.

'Your worships, this is a very serious charge that has been made against my client, but I have to say that there has been no *prima facie* case made against Mr Connelly, let alone one that may be substantiated. The only person who was in the house apart from the accused man was the deceased herself and in her statements, both on oath and to witnesses, she swore that her husband had nothing to do with her being burned.'

Here Mr Atter paused for dramatic effect, and his gaze swept round the room. He now paced a little and held a finger in the air and indulged in some declamation,

'It has been said by the coroner that this was a case where there was some suspicion and I have to say that is right. But where does the suspicion lie? With all due respect to the coroner I have to ask, was there any suspicion whatsoever that can be attached to my client?'

Atter paused again.

'There has been evidence given against Mr Connelly by two drunken men, both of whom admit that they have been in gaol time out of number. These are the only witnesses, I repeat, the only witnesses who have made any accusations against this unfortunate man and even then they have contradicted each other.'

Mr Atter now grew grave.

'We also have the evidence of Sarah Madge.'

A slight buzz of approval was heard in the room.

'Miss Madge stated that these two accusers were not even in the house when the deceased was carried out. Does truth lie in the testimony of these two men, or in the testimony of Sal Madge?'

Edward Atter had now laid the matter before the bench and the public. He could finish it off.

'I submit that all the other evidence bears out the statements made by Mr Connelly and that poor dead woman. No screaming was heard by the neighbours as might have been heard if she had been held on a fire. There were no marks or bruises upon her person apart from the burns and no sign at all of any fight between husband and wife. I will not say that it is not a case that may not be inquired into further...' Here Mr Atter's face assumed a dubious expression and he made a deprecating gesture, 'But there is not one tittle of evidence to justify the accusation which has been made against my client. I ask that he be released at once.'

When Mr Atter sat down widespread murmuring broke out and the magistrates whispered among themselves without retiring.

'Well gentlemen,' said Reverend Fox. 'Given a choice between the word of Sal Madge and the word of those two rascals I have no doubts at all.'

The other two agreed. Without further ado Reverend Fox banged his gavel to call the court to order which happened instantly.

'We find that there is insufficient evidence to proceed with the charges against the prisoner. The prisoner is discharged.'

Reverend Fox banged his gavel down again; there was some cheering in the room and several people slapped John Connelly on the back. He simply sat in a sort of daze for a moment then he stood and shook Edward Atter's hand, thanked him and was led away by some friends. He had a wife to bury and then to mourn. Edward Atter stood in the courtroom and began to gather up his things.

'Well done, Atter,' said Reverend Fox. 'Heaven knows what those scoundrels were at. If this was the assize court they've have been up for perjury, but it's not worth proceeding with at this level.'

'Oh, I fancy that there will be some come back,' replied Atter. 'This is not a town that forgives the sort of thing they have done.'

'But to lie and accuse a man of murder; to try to have him hanged!'

'Well,' said Mr Atter, 'It didn't work. We must leave them to the judgment of God, but if any of them ever come to me for defence, they won't get it.'

Reverend Fox smiled, 'I have to observe that in this town Mr Atter, that of itself is a penalty quite severe in its own nature.'

At about eleven o'clock that night the waves were lapping gently against the stone harbour wall and the night was dry, not too cold, but it was dark. Richard Walker really should have known better than to stay out late on this particular evening; it might have been sensible for him if he had let matters subside and let the volcanic emotions that went with them die down into mere annoyance. Sal Madge was angry, which is really an understatement, for there was a hot fury in her head that she had to do something about or explode, for she had been made out to be a liar in court. She was also a woman of her word and she had made a promise to Richard Walker. Drunk again, he saw her shadowy figure along the edge of the quay and if he had possessed the sense he was born with, he would have run away. His first mistake was that he did not, which was stupid of him. He knew Sal's reputation, but had never seen it in action, so part of him did not believe that she was capable of what he had heard. That was his second mistake; he felt some stirring of trepidation, but it was not enough to stop him; she was, after all, only a woman. He approached to where she stood and made to go past her. She stepped in front of him,

'Whear do you think you're garn?'

'Home, I'm going home. What's it to you?'

Sal stepped close to him and set her face to his.

'You gave me the lie in court twice this week. You're a damned liar.'

'I told what I knew.'

'You telt me you'd tell the truth Dick. You didn't. Because I expect Parker told you not to.'

'Get out of my way; I ain't scared of you.'

'You're more afraid of Parker eh? Big mistake Dick; he's nowt but a laal biddy to be squashed.'

'You going to do that are you? Get out of my way you ugly old gimmer.'

Sal laughed savagely, 'Gimmer eh? Aye that's as may be, but this gimmer made a promise didn't she Dick? Remember?'

He barely had time to realise her intention when her knee came up in his groin and squashed his testicles against his abdomen. He screamed shrill and loud as pure agony lanced across his lower body and an earthquake of pain doubled him over. That was merely the first shock as his body reacted to the hard and accurate impact of a solid bony thud on his privates. The reaction pain made him burst out crying and he gasped for breath, as he had not enough air left to scream the intensity of his anguish. Then he was violently sick and fell on the floor doubled over in a foetal position; pain such as made you wish you had never been born. Sal looked down on him then spat a copious jet of tobacco juice; she was quite unrepentant.

'You call me a liar again you piece of shite and I swear they'll find you in the dock face down.'

With that she turned and walked away. Pounding feet along the quayside signalled the imminent arrival of PC Thomas Beattie. Looking down on the ground Beattie recognised Walker straight away; he would have had no trouble, even if he had not known before today who Walker was; he had become one of the most unpopular men in town in a very short time.

'Oh it's you is it? The drunk that sees things. What's happened to you? I heard screaming.'

'She kicked me in the balls!'

'Oh did she? Who? Some prozzie you wouldn't pay?'

'Sal Madge! She did it. I want her arrested.'

'Sal Madge kicked you in the balls did she?'

Beattie looked around.

'No Sal Madges here. Sure you're not seeing things again?'

'She assaulted me.'

'Aye; like John Connelly held his wife on't fire. Get up and get home before I run you in for being drunk and disorderly.'

Walker saw that he would get nowhere with wanting Sal arrested.

'Give us a hand up.'

'I will not,' said Beattie. 'You're covered in sick; I'm not touching you. Get up and get home before I arrest you. Here comes the wagon now. They'll take you away.'

Walker crawled to his knees, still weeping from pain and used a wall to get to his feet. Stumbling and shambling he went away. Beattie watched him go then chuckled to himself,

'Good for you, lass. Good for you.'

Richard Walker was small fry. Sal Madge's most venomous feelings were reserved firmly for Edward Parker. She had determined that she was not prepared to wait for providence to visit a retribution upon him. The wrath of God was one thing, but the wrath of Sal Madge was something else and a swift knee in the groin was not enough. She did not particularly want to use violence against him for she had given no undertaking to do so. She did, however, wish to tell him what she thought of him and that would give her a great deal of satisfaction. The words she might use chewed over in her mind again and again and she determined that she could not rest easy until she had said them. She could not tell him this night though as he was at home, having spent the day after he left court drinking a lot of beer. Parker was disappointed, but not entirely displeased. The man he conceived of as his enemy had been locked up for a fortnight and dragged through the courts, caused a great deal of pain and Parker was stupid enough to think that he himself had emerged as some sort of hero. In actual fact, he had not; he had drunk alone that night and no one had offered to treat him. In the dirty room he rented in Mount Pleasant he was safe enough; his aversion to hard work ensured his wellbeing during the next day and he sallied forth in the evening to drink some more.

It often takes time for human beings to get organised. Whitehaven had been talking; specifically people had been talking about who they believed and the verdict was almost unanimous. The model of working class integrity, hard work and good fellowship that was Sal Madge was not someone whose word was questioned. Above all there was awe, and in this was rooted the true depth of her legend.

'She went into a house she thought was on fire to save a woman.'

'Aye, and John Kennedy with her.'

'I've been speaking to t'folk in Rosemary Lane; it's exactly how she says it was.'

'She should get a medal. To run into a burning house to rescue that poor woman. I've never heard of owt so brave.'

'I wuz thear; bravest thing ah've ivver sin. All these men standing gawking and she went straight in like it was nowt.'

'The house wasn't burning.'

'Aye, but she thought it was.'

'True enough; she's a heroine; that's what she is.'

'She probably would have got a medal but for that Parker and his marra.'

'Man's a dirty little tick,' and so on multiplied many times in the telling.

As the gossip progressed Sal's status rose like a star into the sky and there it stayed, glowing like a jewel in the night.

Edward Parker was blissfully unaware of this; after he had taken two pints he did not notice at all that people were loath to talk to him. He might have seen that men were watching him warily and with guarded expressions on their faces. He was not having a lot of fun and decided that he would make his way along past the harbour and towards Bardywell Steps. There were places there where he knew more people and he might enjoy himself more. In the shadows, furtive whispering figures followed him, but he did not notice them. If he had been listening he might have heard the rattle of clogs on stone, but he was not.

Sal Madge did not need to be furtive; she had been waiting where West Strand met Quay Street and stood at the entrance to the narrow alley leading to the steps. If she had seen the six shadows she would not have bothered; if they were anything to worry about she would have thought six against her was reasonably good odds. Now Parker saw her, standing in front of him.

'I've been waiting for you, Mr Parker.'

'Tha's got nowt to say that I want to hear you auld biddy. Get the hell out of my way.'

Parker, young, fit and twenty-four advanced towards Sal; she did not get out of the way.

'I said get out of my way you old bitch,' and he went to shove Sal Madge violently out of his way. To his astonishment, as if she knew where he was going to push, she was not there. Next thing he found that both of his feet were swept from under him by one swing of her leg and he landed hard and flat on the cobblestones on his back; all his breath whooshed out of him and he lay there with the most complete look of surprise on his face. Sal stood above him, looked at him right in the eye and said, 'If you know what's good for tha, you'll stop there.'

Her jaws were chewing and as she looked at him she spat, deliberately, a stream of brown tobacco juice onto the floor beside him. Gasping air back into his lungs he looked at her, and for the first time he knew fear; perhaps the stories he had heard about her were true.

'You're a dirty flea-bitten son of a poxed bitch,' said Sal Madge pleasantly. 'Your Mam would have done the world a favour if she'd chucked you in the harbour when you were born and the world would have one less piece of shite to worry about. Even better if thy Dad had had a wank instead then there would have been no trouble for anyone.'

'Eh, you can't talk to me like that!' said Parker.

'I'm doing it,' replied Sal. 'You lied in the coroner's court on oath and you did it again in the police court. You're a damned liar, a lousy scabby bit of a slug that tries to pass as a man. You ain't worth the time or the breath to kick, so I can't be bothered to put thy lights out. Now I've got some advice for thee.'

'I don't want your bloody advice.'

'You should,' replied Sal. 'I think you should get out of town and not come back.'

Parker scoffed. 'Why the hell should I do that? Fear of you?'

Sal leaned closer in, 'Oh believe me sonny, if I wanted to make you fear me, you'd fear me. Nay; life's too short and I have no time for you.' At the last bit he almost reeled back from the contempt in her face. 'The dogshit on my shoe is worth more than you. Cross me again, you'll answer for it.'

With that she walked away.

He stared after her for a minute, then sneered and started to get up.

'Don't bother getting up; you'll only be going back down again.'

Startled, Parker looked round behind him; six men came out of the shadows; each had a kerchief tied round their faces. Their leader came forward.

'She's a decent human being is Sal Madge, brave as a lion, and she gave you good advice. Trouble is that she's too late. Why is that marras?'

Here he turned to look at the men beside him.

'Because it's too late,' replied one of them in a joyful tone.

'Exactly so,' said the leader. 'You should have got out straight after the trial. You're not liked around here Parker.'

The last sentence was thrown with real force. They could smell his fear now.

'What do you want?'

The leader ignored him, 'Not the head marras; and try not to put him in hospital; this time.'

'What do you mean?' said Parker, trying to get up but being shoved down by one of the men.

The leader called out to another man further out on Quay Street.

'Where's PC Beattie?'

'Other end of his beat.'

'Plenty of time then,' said the leader and slapped Parker's face hard.

Parker opened his mouth to yell, but as soon as he did so a large piece of cotton waste was shoved into it and his sound was cut off as it formed in his throat.

'They always open their mouths when you slap their faces,' said the leader, as if giving his pupils instruction.

Then they began to kick him with their clogged feet. They knew what they were doing. They did not kick his head or his ribs, but every soft part of his body was targeted and he cowered on the ground whimpering, then crying as the blows came in. Rather to his surprise, they stopped after about three minutes and the leader stooped close and snarled into his ear.

'That was a sample. If you're still in town in two days you'll be in the infirmary on the third day. If you're still here after that then you might be found in a wooden box if anyone cares to look, which I doubt. Thou shalt not bear false witness against thy neighbour. We don't like thy sort in Whitehaven. Think on it. Oh, and speaking of dog shit.'

Two men grabbed Parker's face and forced it down into some dog turds lying on the cobbles; they rubbed his face in it as he squealed, then walked off down the hill laughing.

'Next time you'll be eating it,' the leader called over his shoulder as he strode away.

There was no next time. The morning found a bruised Parker at the station, all he possessed in a bag, catching an early workman's train south. Where he went and what happened to him, nobody cared, least of all Sal Madge, now seen as an ornament and a decoration to her town, a status she was to enjoy for the rest of her life.

Chapter 16

Epilogue

Sal Madge, as everyone knew, never missed a day of work. Rain or shine, frost, snow and gale, she was out there on the wagon way leading her horse and taking coals to the incline. It seemed that somehow she had come to embody the hard working and spirited grit of the town; a kind of personification of Whitehaven itself. Tough, getting on a bit, slightly dirty and smelly, but full of character and guts, she was an admirable metaphor for the place, so people were proud of her, and proud of the town. The truth was though that she never claimed to be anything special, and she was all too human. At fifty-nine she seemed impervious to the vagaries of life, as if she were made of oak; but she was not.

Thursday 20 March 1890 was a blustery day and the wind gusted to gale force, playing mischief with the ships in the harbour, lifting loose objects and slamming doors throughout the town. At the top of the Howgill incline some wagons had just been hauled up and run onto the turntable, which was done two at a time. From there they could be easily pushed onto the return line for empty wagons; Sal had helped do this manoeuvre thousands of time. She was chatting away to Bill Calhoun and putting her shoulder to the wagons to shift them when a blast of wind caught them; they had not been braked, and they rolled as the turntable turned. One of them came off the rails with the force of the wind and it leaned over against its guardrails, pinning Sal between. The weight of the wagon tipped onto her and her hip was slammed against the guardrail. Being Sal she did not scream, but grunted in pain and shouted gruffly at her marras around.

'Help; get this bloody thing off me.'

'Pandemonium broke loose and at least twelve men dropped what they were doing at the head of the incline; they grabbed the wagon and heaved it off her by sheer brute force, while two of them dragged Sal away to the side.

'Can you get up Sal? Does it hurt.'

'Aye, it bloody hurts. What do you think? I can feel it swelling up like hell.'

'Can you walk?'

Sal Madge made to try to get up, then grimaced with the pain.

'Sorry Marra; I can't.'

They put her onto a stretcher and carried her down the incline, where she did not have to suffer the indignity of being carried through the town. The manager of the incline, Mr Shackley, sent for a cab which caused Sal great concern. She had never been in a cab and did not want to pay for one now.

'Don't you worry about cost, lass; I'll not be out of pocket and nor will you. Now let's get thou to the infirmary.'

She was taken away at a gentle pace leaving her workmates shaking their heads in disbelief.

'Did you see that? Damn great wagon tipped on her, full weight of it on her hip, and not a bloody squeak!'

'That's Sal for you. I'd have been yelling my head off!'

'She was sweating a bit.'

'Wouldn't thou be sweating a bit with that lot on you?'

'Well you can say what you like; I've not seen owt like that. She's got guts right enough.'

'You're in the right of it there marra; enough guts for six.'

'Course she has. That's Sal Madge for you!'

'Will she be alright do you think?'

'Aye of course she will. She'll do what she always does when she's got a problem.'

'What's that then?'

'Kick it in the balls of course!'

This caused a general laugh; of course Sal would be fine. She always was.

It was Dr Irwin who examined her. He was well used to folk who did not wash, and he did not wince. Instead he told the nurses to remove Sal's clothes for examination, then he looked at her hip which had gone dark blue and swelled up nastily.

'This is going to hurt.'

'I know it is: get on with it,' she managed through gritted teeth.

She suffered him to poke at it, prod it and palpate the hip without a murmur though sweat appeared on her brow.

'Very well,' said Dr Irwin. 'I do not believe that it is broken, but it has been very seriously crushed and horribly bruised. You will have to stay here I'm afraid until it gets better.'

'How long will that be?'

'About a month, I should think. Your age will make it slower to heal than in a younger woman. You'll probably be on your feet before that but unable to work. I think it best you stay in. No Miss Madge; no arguments. There is one doctor in this room and it is me.'

Sal made a moue with her mouth, but she was in no position to do anything about it.

'Nurse.'

'Yes Doctor?'

'A bed bath please; a very good one.'

'Of course doctor,' replied the nurse grimly.

Thereafter Sal remembered her time in hospital as being quite nice for the food and the warmth, but the baths as being an unnecessary inconvenience. It was not long before Isaac Tyson came to see her bringing her flowers.

'You're not supposed to bring those; they're not good for the patients,' said the rather pretty nurse.

'Daffs?' said Sal. 'How are they bad for me? They're my favourite is daffs.'

'Germs,' said the nurse laconically. 'They're against the rules. Doctor will throw a fit.'

'Oh well lass, we couldn't have that now could we?' said Sal, taking the flowers from Isaac with a thank you. 'I think you'd better have them.'

With a wink to Isaac she handed the flowers to the nurse who was completely taken aback, went red, then took the flowers.

'Thank you, Miss Madge. I'd better go and put them in water in the nurse's room.'

Isaac laughed, 'Well you've set her all a fluster, Sal.'

'I'm fifty-nine years old Isaac. I've noticed that I have that effect on some of them occasionally.'

Isaac looked at her wryly, the only man who could talk to her this way, 'You're not like them though, are you?'

175

'No, I'm not,' said Sal. 'I'm nowt like them.' Then she thought for a minute. 'Hest thou got Flirt?'

'I have. He's in the house and the grandchildren are spoiling him rotten.'

'That's good. He's cracking on a bit and could do with a bit of spoiling.'

Isaac looked at her long and steady then said slowly, 'I might have something to say about that to you, Sal. Not yet; we'll let you get a bit better first, but Flirt isn't the only one who's cracking on a bit.'

'What do you mean?'

'You'll see in time. You've a few weeks in here and I've got a few things to see to.'

'Concerning me?'

'Aye, concerning you. But I'll speak when I'm ready.'

'I ain't retiring if that's what you mean. I have to graft,'

'You retire? That'll be the day! No, I can't see you retiring. You'd run mad if you had no work. Like I said, I'll tell you my mind when I'm ready.'

She knew him well enough to know that protest would not get any more out of him, so she left the matter where it was. It is not the Cumbrian way to press when a man declares he has said his piece.

To her the next few weeks were oppressive. The only good thing was that the place was warm, meals were regular and she was well looked after; slowly she healed with a regime of hot and cold poultices and warm baths. The baths were thought to be very therapeutic in bringing out the bruising, but it was a full two weeks before they let her out of bed and then only with a crutch. To look at her during that time, nobody would have been able to say 'as black as Sal Madge' for she was clean and neat; as she wanted her hair to stay short, the nurses trimmed it for her. When she did get out of bed she knew that the doctor had been right; she was not fit for work, so she had to be content to hobble round the hospital until she could at least pretend to walk normally. She had a stream of visitors of course, and not only from her own walk in life either. All sorts of people dropped in with small gifts of sweets, tobacco and so on; but to her disgust she was not allowed to chew her tobacco or to smoke in the infirmary. To her great surprise Edward Atter came in one day; he only stayed for a few minutes, as they were not really on a conversational level. He merely asked her how she was going on and hoped that she would be recovered soon. Actions sometimes speak louder than words though, and Mr Atter had left a large beefsteak with the infirmary kitchen with the instruction that it should be served to Miss Madge; it was good for building blood and would aid her recovery. Since he was on the infirmary's Board of Governors, his instructions were followed to the letter and Miss Madge, who liked her steak well done, pronounced it to be excellent.

Isaac Tyson had been a daily visitor of course, sometimes with his wife, sometimes with one of his grown up children or grandchildren. Sal had family members who dropped in as well, but after a life of hard work up on the brow she was beginning to feel as if she was in prison and longing to get out and do some hard graft. It was in the third week, when she was hobbling round using a stick that Isaac brought up the subject of her work. By now, he had risen to senior under manager at Wellington pit and was a man of some influence, which he had used to great effect.

'Sal, I've summat to tell you and I want you to listen carefully, for I do not want you to take it the wrong way.'

'Alright. I'm listening. What is it?'

'Well first of all, there's a lot of folk hold you in regard; you've a lot of friends in this town.'

'That's nice to know.'

'Aye well, they've been concerned about you. You know Sal you're like me; cracking on a bit and everyone's a bit worried about you.'

'I'm alright. I'm getting better every day. I'll be back up top before you can say Jack Robinson, never you fear.'

'That's just it Sal. You won't.'

'What do you mean, I won't? I've got to work, haven't I?'

'Yis I know that, lass. Without work you'd shrink up and fade away. Haven't I seen you on that wagon way for the last fifty years? Nay, you'll not be out along there any more. It was a hard winter last year and you were getting soaked, frozen, blown inside out and I don't know what. Fact is that at our age we need to take a little more care of ourselves.'

'I've never been ill. Until now I've never taken a day off work; you can't say I shirk.'

'God no; no one could ever say that about you! No, the fact is that I've put in a word and you've been promoted.'

'Promoted? To what?' Sal was deeply suspicious.

'Nay, don't take on. You'll remember Ezra?'

'Of course I bloody do; I see him every damned day. What sort of question is that?'

Ezra Tinnion was the occupant of the brake hut at the top of the Howgill incline. His job was twofold. When a wagonload of coal had been attached and was ready to be lowered to the hurries on the harbourside, Ezra had to operate a semaphore telegraph which communicated with John Bellringer in the hut at the bottom of the incline. This signified that he was ready. When Bellringer signalled that all was well, Ezra pulled a lever that allowed the wagon to go down the inclined plane as it slowly drew up four empty wagons from below.

'Do you know how old he is?'

'No,' said Sal. 'I don't. He's been there for ever.'

'Have a guess.'

'Sixty eight?'

'Try eighty five.'

Sal's mouth opened in disbelief, 'Well I take my hat off! That's a good stint.'

'Aye it is; and he's got rheumatism. His daughter's been at him to step down for a long time now and he's decided to call it a day.'

'What's he going to live on?'

'He's been paying into a mutual for years; don't have any fears on that. And he'll get a Lonsdale pension for his longer service. Mr Dee the agent will see to that, don't you fret. Anyway you've got his job.'

'I have?'

'Aye, Sal. It's time you took things a bit easier. No reason you shouldn't stay doing that job as long as you like.'

Sal mused, 'It's a bit of a soft number.'

Isaac laughed, 'There's no doubt of that. Nice coal stove in the hut in the winter with a kettle bubbling on it. Windows open in summer. Oh and a fine view across the town.'

'I'd see everyone I know.'

'You would; every working day. Oh, and did I say; five bob a week more than you're getting now.'

'What about heaving wagons?'

'No more of that. Responsible job and all that. Ezra's staying until you can come and take over. Start Monday; can you manage it?'

'Let them try and stop me!'

So it was that Sal spent the next nine years operating the telegraph and brake at the Howgill incline where she had worked for so many years. Her habits stayed as they had always been; she liked her beer, her aging dog, and loved her pipe and chewing baccy. Flirt died in 1897 and although it upset her she was phlegmatic; she was too close to the earth to make a great demonstration of sorrow. The order of things is to be born, to live and then to die; she knew that, but like a lot of humanity she had a central feeling of her own immortality. She grew older and acquired more wrinkles; once again, 'as black as Sal Madge' meant something around town. She would arm wrestle men still and on many occasions she was the victor. To outward appearance she was as hale and hearty as she had ever been as she approached her sixty-eighth year.

It was on Saturday 1 April 1899 that she fell ill with a cough; her friends at first thought that she was playing an April Fool trick on them when she did not turn up to work, for it was unheard of for her to be ill. Running a high temperature with a very sore throat and coughing up blood, she took to her bed and did no work for the first time in over half a century apart from her time in the infirmary. The truth was that she had been suffering an irritation in her throat for some weeks, but had shrugged it off as a cold. When the doctor came he made a very quick diagnosis; she had been suffering from bronchitis, not a cold, and it had spread to both her lungs as an acute infection. She now had pneumonia. There was no point in taking her to the infirmary, as they could do nothing that could not be done at home. There was no medicine to help her; all she could do was to stay in bed and fight it out.

Sal had help, of course; there were friends, neighbours and the other people in the house, and she did fight it but to no avail. Her nephew John's wife did most of the nursing, but although Ann Madge did her best with broths and poultices, Sal did not improve. Her breathing grew shallow, her pulse rapid and she spent much of her time asleep which was a mercy. On Friday 7 April her heart stopped while she slept, so she passed peacefully and unconsciously from the world, a victim to the disease which killed many in her community and which was known by the nickname of 'old man's friend.' On her death it was found that there was insufficient money to bury her; it would have to be done at the expense of the ward she lived in. She was not, however, to have a pauper's funeral; as it turned out hers would be unique; a people's funeral.

The news of her death spread round the town like the shockwaves of an eruption. In a time where the average age of death for a working man was fifty-two, many in the town had lived their entire lives at the same time as Sal Madge. That such a character was gone from them was almost incomprehensible; surely she was invincible and simply could not be gone. She lay in Mark Lane until the afternoon of Monday 10 April and it became known that the funeral would take place then. Huge crowds gathered round the area of Mark Lane and a hush fell as a simple wooden coffin was brought out of number six. On its lid was a small cross, made of bright yellow daffodils; no one knew who put it there, though there was much speculation. As the cortege moved away down Mark Lane and onto Strand Street a surge of people followed, bare headed and silent. Many of the shops that it passed put up closed signs and the owners and staff left, so that they could follow the procession. The conversation in MA Batty's confectioner's shop in Lowther Street was typical,

'Mr Batty, they're burying Sal Madge this afternoon.'

'Aye lass, I know. You want to go?'

'I'd like to.'

'So would I. Lock the door and let's all go.'

Turning down into Swingpump Lane, the cart carrying the small coffin was followed by an estimated two thousand people as Whitehaven turned out to say its farewell. As they slowly passed on their way they approached an elderly man standing on the pavement who took off his cap. He turned, in some mystification to his neighbour, a gentleman in a top hat, who stood with a lady, evidently his wife.

'Excuse me, marra. Ah's frae Wukiton and I don't knaw what's garn on here. Who are they burying? A king or a queen?'

Edward Atter turned to his questioner, 'A queen? I think that is probably not an inaccurate statement as far as Whitehaven is concerned. Yes indeed; you might very well say that.'

Mr Atter had finally married Miss Cameron and their marriage had prospered; they dwelt in a fine big house, Glen Ard, on Inkerman Terrace. As the coffin passed, Mr Atter took off his hat, then with Mrs Atter on his arm, swung in behind to follow it out along the Low Road towards the cemetery. Strung out on the road towards Sal's final resting place the procession looked for all the world like the burial cortege of a monarch or a duke. Whitehaven gave Sal Madge its own equivalent of a state funeral and it was heartfelt. The whole universe may be contained within the mind of God and the lives of planets and stars, all life may be nothing more than passing thoughts, though some flash brighter than others; she was one such and all knew it.

They laid her to rest surrounded by a multitude of people whose sorrow and respect was palpable. The mark of a person's worth may in a great measure be gauged by the esteem with which they are regarded in the world. Sal was no great beauty, made no wonderful marriage and had no children; she won no great battles; she did not travel outside the town where she was brought up, wrote no books and made no fortune. Yet in the common herd of humanity she stood out like a pearl from the muddy mussel and did much good in her time. Whitehaven buried one of their own and mourned her passing, but she lived on in their hearts and minds as someone remarkable and of admirable qualities; that is no bad epitaph. The final testimony of Sal Madge was in the crowds at her graveside; it may have been mute, but it was eloquent, and witness to a life fulfilled and lived well.

Printed in Great Britain
by Amazon